ROOT OF PASSION

ANN ROBERTS

Bella
BOOKS

2009

Bella Books, Inc.
P.O. Box 10543
Tallahassee, FL 32302

Printed in the United States of America on acid-free paper
First Edition

Editor: Katherine V. Forrest
Cover Designer: Stephanie Solomon-Lopez

ISBN 10: 1-59493-155-0
ISBN 13:978-1-59493-155-0

Dedication

I spend an excessive amount of time living in my head, caught in my own fantasy world, creating characters and constructing dialogue. My partner Amy is indeed the most patient person I know. She has endured many conversations where my attention drifts to my latest story and I'm reduced to a grunting, distracted blob. Yet, she still loves me and nurtures my creative side. I am a very lucky woman.

Acknowledgments

It is an honor to have Katherine V. Forrest as my editor, and I am truly grateful for her advice and insight. I am also thankful to Karin Kallmaker who made some key suggestions during the early brainstorming stages and helped the story evolve. And of course, without the continued support of Linda Hill and Bella, my words and ideas would just be a file in my computer.

An enormous thanks to all of the readers who continue to support the publishing industry by spending their hard-earned cash on our books. I certainly appreciate it. *Root of Passion* requires readers to ask, "What if?" and suspend their understanding of reality. It's a novel of escape, and hopefully, in these hard economic times, you'll think that's a good thing.

"The wilderness holds answers to more questions than we
have yet learned to ask."
- Nancy Newhall

About the Author

Ann Roberts is the author of *Furthest from the Gate, Brilliant, Beach Town,* and the Ari Adams' mystery series which includes *Paid in Full* and *White Offerings.* She lives in Arizona with her family.

Chapter 1

Somewhere in South America...

Margo wandered through the marketplace, past a gauntlet of vendors peddling everything from wicker baskets to fresh chickens. The haggling voices ranged from simple questioning to downright belligerence as the customers and sellers engaged in the inevitable tug-of-war bartering that was the staple of commerce in this part of the world. Margo understood little, since she didn't speak Portuguese. She lingered at a sweets stand, breathing in the pleasant odor of cinnamon. She didn't buy anything, having suffered a terrible case of food poisoning the last time she sampled some irresistible meat wraps from a street seller in Korea.

She ignored most of the wares and goods that surrounded her. She rarely purchased trinkets; however, when she did find something amazing, she snatched it up quickly and became the envy of her friends back home, who couldn't believe the bargains she found during her layovers.

As a flight attendant for United Airlines, she traveled the world and enjoyed visiting the exotic locales, but she seldom stayed in any place for more than a day or two. Regions blurred together, and while she would never mistake Europe for the Sudan, if asked later where she'd traveled that week, she'd simply respond, "Somewhere in South America, Rio de Janeiro, I think."

Three of the other crew members had enticed her to join them as they explored Rio. At first Margo had balked, hesitant to be sandwiched in a Jeep between Connor the pilot and Jeanette the copilot. She was sleeping with both of them, but she was rather certain neither suspected the other was part of a romantic triangle. Her best friend Grace was appalled by her bed-hopping, but she was who she was—always playing the odds, if it served her purposes. She'd only found herself in a few tight situations, but she'd managed to avoid the vengeful type of girlfriend and boyfriend who would pour acid on her car or send her dead flowers.

Her luck was certainly being tested on this trip. She was floored when she learned she'd be working the same flight with both of her current lovers. Fortunately, Connor, a stately man approaching fifty, enjoyed a simple dinner and a romp in the sack while Jeanette was a wild woman whose evenings didn't begin until eleven. She could easily satisfy both of them, and her own fatigue was worth it. *Ah, the stress of bisexuality.*

She stopped and looked around, realizing that she'd absently turned a corner and the raucous noise of the vendors was behind her. Her co-workers were nowhere in sight and she was alone in a narrow alley, the buildings on both sides so close that shadows sheltered the cobblestones. All of the structures were decrepit, and Margo thought if she pressed her palm against the wooden frames, each building would fall into a heap, like tumbling dominoes.

Shabby windows stared at her, each pane covered with black

and white drawings—dark eyes preventing the sliver of sunlight to enter. Her morbid curiosity beckoned her to explore, and she glanced at each window that she passed. Some of the symbols she recognized—pentagrams, astrological signs, skulls and scythes, but most were mysterious and strange. None conveyed warmth or friendliness. She passed a large window depicting the grim reaper standing over a skeleton, his scythe pressed against his victim's ribcage. She shivered and stepped backward, deciding to return to the main street and the comfort of the crowded marketplace.

A rusty hinge moaned behind her, and she turned to see an emerald green door, just slightly ajar. How did she miss that? She hadn't noticed any doors along the alley, but she'd been focused on the artwork in the windows, so she rationalized that her eyes had absently tripped past it.

Naturally curious and not easily spooked, she opened the door slowly, and the scent of vanilla overwhelmed her. She smiled. It was exactly like her grandmother's kitchen when she was a child. Grandma was always baking, and every Sunday when Margo entered the old lady's house, happiness wrapped around her. It was probably the reason vanilla was still her favorite scent.

She navigated a short hallway into a room filled with dozens of shelves, each lined with rows of unique bottles, carafes and vessels filled with colored liquid. It was a stark contrast to the dreariness of the alley, and she turned a full three hundred and sixty degrees, gazing at the reds, blues, pinks, yellows and oranges. For a moment, she had the odd feeling that she'd stumbled into a Saturday morning cartoon.

She stepped toward a shelf and studied the beautiful containers that held the liquids. No two were alike—different heights, shapes and designs. Her eyes were drawn to a carafe shaped like a swan filled with golden fluid. The color embellished the fine cuts in the glass, and she automatically picked it up without thinking. It was heavier than she thought, and she wondered if it was carved from lead crystal. Her fingers traced the beautiful form and brushed against a metal band affixed to the bottom. It was a label inscribed with the words, *Potion of Grace*.

She suddenly felt as if she was being watched. She whirled around, the swan nearly slipping from her fingers.

"Please don't drop that. You could never replace it."

She faced a goddess. The young woman, probably no older than twenty-four, wore a white gauze dress that clung to her curves, and Margo could see the outline of her firm breasts through the sheer material. Her eyes were dark, and her wavy black hair flowed over her shoulders. She studied Margo, saying nothing for a long time, as if she was sizing her up.

Eventually she smiled. "Welcome. I am Chayna," she said softly, her English perfect.

Margo wondered if she was American, since there wasn't a trace of an accent in her voice, but her rich olive skin suggested she was a native.

"Hello," she said, replacing the swan carefully on the shelf. "This is a remarkable store. What's in the bottles?"

"Everything a person could want."

Too paranoid to reach for the carafe again, she pointed at the swan. "That one's labeled Potion of Grace. What does it mean?"

"As the name implies, it helps those who are, shall we say, more likely to struggle with klutziness."

She gazed at the bottle. "That's why it's displayed in a swan, isn't it? Swans are very graceful."

Chayna nodded. "Exactly." She gestured to a shelf dominated by tall, thin bottles. "This section is reserved for self-esteem—improved confidence, candor and humor."

Margo raised an eyebrow. "That little potion can help someone be funnier? Really?"

Chayna shrugged. "I've never had a complaint."

"If that's true, then I know about a thousand comedians who would love this shop."

Both of them laughed and Margo's gaze settled on a shelf behind the exotic saleswoman, to a heart-shaped bottle filled with rich, lavender liquid and two glass doves perched at the center.

"What's that one?"

"Ah, that's the Root of Passion."

Chayna carefully lifted the bottle with both hands and placed it on the counter. She gently pulled at the doves, and Margo realized they acted as a beautiful stopper. She leaned closer, unable to believe what she was seeing. The contents were moving. She watched the lavender liquid swirl inside the bottle, and, for a moment, she could have sworn the deep red and cerulean blue separated and remixed.

"The Root of Passion pierces the heart and frees a person of his or her sexual inhibitions."

She snorted. "I certainly don't need that."

Chayna arched her eyebrows. "Really?"

She gazed at Chayna, and a wave of heat surged through her. "No."

"Well, it doesn't matter. You can't buy anything in this store for yourself. It would be a waste of money. Do you see the sign?"

She glanced up to a simple white paper that hung above the doorway. *FOR A GIFT.*

"So people don't buy anything for themselves?" she asked, unable to believe that such a rule existed.

"No, only to give to others."

"How do you know? What if customers try to use it?"

"I know that the powers of the potions are affected by the receiver's energy. You have been here and have one kind of energy. The potions won't work for you as the giver; however, should you purchase one for a friend in need, he or she will feel the full effects."

She contemplated the theory. She couldn't imagine how it would be any different if she were to drink a potion or give it to a friend, perhaps Grace. *Grace could certainly use the Root of Passion,* she thought. But the possibility of Grace, a surgeon, imbibing anything not approved by the FDA was unthinkable. Ironically, she herself would have no hesitation grabbing the bottle and swallowing a few mouthfuls. That realization confounded her.

Where is your sense of caution, Margo? You're standing in a ramshackle store in a foreign country talking to a woman who says she has magic elixirs that can cure the individual ills of society. Are you nuts? How about throwing back a few ounces of bleach, too?

"You seem drawn to the Root of Passion," Chayna concluded. "Do you know anyone who might benefit from such a potion?"

"My friend, Grace. But I couldn't get her to drink it. She's a doctor."

"Ah, I see your predicament, but I imagine with the right level of persuasion, she could be enticed to try it. And," she added, shaking the beautiful bottle, "the root itself has its own magnetic qualities."

They both watched the beautiful lavender swirl in the bottle. It seemed to move clockwise, and the effect was hypnotic. Eventually the liquid resettled, but Margo's eyes remained glued to the bottle.

"Do you see?"

"Yes." she nodded. "I'd like to buy some. What's the price?"

"One hundred dollars for one vial. And I will only sell you one potion. Are you sure you want this one?"

She glanced at the shelves, but her gaze quickly returned to the Root of Passion. She'd just have to persuade Grace to try it. *It'll be okay.*

"How much does she need to drink?"

"Just a sip whenever she wants to heighten her sexual senses or free herself of her inhibitions."

Chayna went behind the counter and withdrew a small oak box. She undid the clasp, and Margo saw that the box was filled with sawdust, cushioning a vial. Once the liquid was transferred, she carefully replaced the vial in the box.

Margo stared at the large bottle, the contents swirling furiously from being upended. She watched until the reds and blues resettled into their lavender state, and she had an epiphany, a moment of clarity unlike any in her life. She saw a laughing face with dark ringlets dangling on her forehead—Rose. Amid her laughter was an air of surprise, for Rose had little to laugh about, and it was always unexpected when it happened. Margo loved Rose's bright side.

"Are you sure you wouldn't give me one more vial? I'd pay you double."

Chayna smiled at what Margo was sure was a common question. "That would be against store policy."

She leaned over the counter, resting her hands on the beautiful bottle. "And, undoubtedly, you'd be fired for violating the rules."

Chayna placed her warm hands over Margo's. "I shouldn't," she said simply.

"But you will."

Her eyes narrowed. "I will, because I can tell that you *need* it. You *want* the first vial, but you *crave* the second." She came from behind the counter. Her lithe body stretched across the shelves, moving several carafes, obviously looking for something. The muscles in her back rippled underneath the sheer fabric of her dress, and Margo imagined her naked.

When she turned around, it appeared she held a small bicycle tire, and Margo was confused. She returned to the counter and Margo realized the tire was, in fact, a circular glass tube about a foot in diameter filled with black liquid.

She placed the tube in a wooden cradle and plucked the cork stopper from the top. Without a word, she withdrew a tacky souvenir that said, "Come to Las Vegas" in blue lettering, from underneath the counter. Carefully she poured a small amount of the liquid into the ceramic coffee mug.

She held up the mug. "Drink this."

Margo blinked in shock. "What?"

"If you drink this, I will give you another vial of the Root of Passion, for free."

She gazed into the mug and sniffed. Nothing. She swirled the liquid, hoping to elicit some similar reaction as the Root of Passion. Nothing. She glanced at Chayna, whose expression was unreadable.

"What is this for? What does it do?"

"You need it," she said.

I need it? What do you do now, Margo? This stuff isn't nearly as appealing as the Root of Passion. Black equals death. Black equals darkness. What if she's feeding you poison? Just because she's incredibly beautiful doesn't mean she isn't capable of murder.

She glanced at the Root of Passion and the beautiful doves perched on the top. Everything suddenly seemed all right. She brought the mug to her lips, and, just as she had taken medicine as a child, she downed the liquid in two swallows. She grasped the counter and waited, worrying she would fall to the floor in a heap.

Chayna filled another vial of the Root of Passion and presented the box. "Your friend is very lucky to have you in her life."

As Margo handed over five twenties, she thought, *She's either lucky, or I'm a sucker for a gorgeous woman.*

Chapter Two

"Number ten, please."

The cold, sleek steel greeted Grace's palm, and she drew the scalpel across Chester Brown's neck. She exposed the artery and began the common procedure of a carotid endarterectomy. Her eyes and hands worked in tandem, manipulating the instruments and directing her team. She inserted a stent to hold the artery open while she removed a buildup of plaque from the inner lining of the artery wall.

No matter how many times she operated, she always marveled at the human body. As a vascular surgeon, she lived in awe of the tiny network of arteries and capillaries that were the freeway of circulation and a network for life. Years of training and hundreds of hours spent studying in the library, poring over tens of thousands of pages of medical tomes culminated in the fluid and intricate movements that saved her patients' lives and earned her a position as a respected medical doctor.

"Grace, his pressure's dropping," Eva, the trauma nurse, warned.

She glanced up at the monitor and barked a series of orders that sent the other team members scurrying around the operating room to comply with her demands.

"Dr. Owens, are you sure we should continue?" the anesthesiologist asked.

She took a deep breath and read the monitors. They had just found the blockage, and they could still turn back. Yet, if she cancelled the procedure, one that was critical for his survival, she'd have to reschedule and subject him to another round of anesthesia. She looked at his face. He still seemed to smile at her under the cloak of drugs. He was seventy-two, and every trip into the OR could be his last.

"Let's proceed," she said, glancing into Eva's brown eyes.

She refocused her concentration, silencing the extraneous noises around her. Successful surgery combined the standard textbook procedure with a keen sensitivity to the innate differences of the human body. Everyone was the same, and, yet, everyone was unique. A good surgeon individualized each procedure for each patient. Natural talent also helped—and sometimes saved the day.

An hour later she greeted Edna Brown and two of the children in the family waiting area of St. Benedict's Hospital. Although Edna wore her perpetual smile, Grace could see the worry behind her eyes. She touched her shoulder gently. "It was rough there for a minute, but he's fine and he's resting now."

Edna pulled her into an embrace. "Thank you so much, Dr. Owens. I don't know how I would live without him." She fished a tissue from her purse and dabbed her eyes.

Grace smiled, exhausted. "You're welcome, Edna. The nurses will let you know when you can go in."

Edna gripped her hand tightly. "God bless you, Dr. Owens. You're an extraordinary woman."

She nodded at the family and headed down the hallway toward the doctor's lounge, somewhat stunned by the comment. Family members routinely thanked her after surgery, but no one ever referred to her as *extraordinary*. In fact, most of her friends would probably agree that she was quite the opposite—extra ordinary. They often kidded her about her mundane life, sometimes to the point where she wanted to shout in their faces, "I'm a respected doctor! Every day I get out of bed, knowing that by the end of the day I will have saved a life or possibly killed someone, a person who depended on me. I feel pressure that you will never understand."

But she couldn't explain her world to anyone else. She was a true Gemini, a two-sided paradox with a curtain between her personalities. She felt it was necessary to protect herself—from herself. She knew the only way she could routinely face the daily life-and-death decisions with a galvanized consciousness was to balance her difficult occupation with a steady and predictable home life.

The workweek drained her of courage and waywardness. She envied those who lived with abandon, jumped into relationships based on their gut feeling, visited exotic places and rarely thought of the long-term consequences when making decisions. She yearned to expand her so-called horizons, but she worried the price would come in the operating room, at a moment when she needed to make a split-second, bold decision.

In a recurring nightmare, she'd just completed a skydiving lesson when her pager went off, summoning her to the hospital. Suddenly she was standing over a patient, repairing his aorta, and he flatlined. She stared at the monitor, watching the horizontal green line and hearing the monotonous beeping—and did nothing. Her staff yelled at her, begging for direction, but she stood frozen over the dying man, holding the metal instruments in her useless hands. She looked down apathetically at the corpse and dropped the tools into his open chest cavity. Then she usually woke up, drenched in sweat, her entire body shaking. It was a premonition, a warning. And she knew to heed it.

She went back through the trauma ward toward the doctor's changing room and noticed Eva leaning over the counter at the nurse's station. She was gesturing, probably telling a humorous story. Eva Castillo was known for her endless ER anecdotes, all of which she picked up from her first nursing gig in South Central Los Angeles, her hometown. She'd seen more shootings, stabbings and overdoses in those two years than Grace had experienced throughout her entire ten year career. And as Eva's former girlfriend, she'd heard all of her stories—several times.

Their eyes met for a second as she passed, and she nodded before looking away. Somehow they'd managed to remain professional even after the breakup last year, not only working in the same hospital, but frequently the same OR. Eva was the top surgical nurse at St. Benedict's and, despite their past, Grace's anxiety lessened whenever she saw Eva's dark brown eyes staring at her from above her surgical mask.

"Grace."

She turned back, hoping she didn't look too eager. She'd taken the breakup quite hard, and instead of moving on she'd chosen to sweep the relationship into a corner and ignore her feelings, burying herself deeper into her work. At least that's what Margo had told her.

"Hey."

"That was really good today. I wasn't sure how that one was going to end."

"I wasn't sure either. It was a lot of teamwork."

Eva shook her head and chuckled. "There wasn't anything *team* about it. You called the shots and we just followed. You were really bold and took a risk. It was gutsy to keep going. When it comes to your job, you know just what to do, when to take a chance," she added.

"So, are you saying I don't know what to do in my *personal* life? I'm just competent professionally?"

Eva sighed and looked away, obviously trying to respond carefully. Grace's gaze settled on her strong arms, muscular from her morning rowing sessions. She knew that under the baggy scrubs was an incredible body that had activated her libido any time Eva stripped off her clothes, which was frequently, since she enjoyed sex immensely. *She enjoys everything. That's why you have nothing in common with her.*

"Look, Grace, it just slipped out. I'm not trying to start anything here. I was just complimenting you."

Eva walked away, leaving her speechless. She felt instantly embarrassed about her response to Eva's innocent comment. But was it so innocent? *She said what was really on her mind, even if she didn't mean to.*

Grace quickly changed, made her rounds and two hours later headed to the doctor's parking garage. By the time she settled into the BMW's leather seat her bones felt heavy, and she could barely turn the ignition over. She hated long surgeries, although she never noticed the fatigue while she operated. It remained in a holding pattern, exploding once she'd exited the OR and returned to the routine of work.

She lowered the windows, enjoying the cool October weather. The terrible summer heat had finally broken and the car no longer felt like a sauna each time she climbed in. Phoenicians were finally reaping some dividends for enduring triple-digit temperatures for three months.

She checked her watch, noticing that she would be late for dinner with Margo. She longed for a hot tub and a glass of merlot. Yet calling and canceling on her best friend would be more effort than it was worth.

"Just go," she muttered.

She found Margo already in a booth in their favorite restaurant, the Monastery. Always ready to lead her down the path of sin, Margo had ordered a glass of merlot for her and she quickly took a sip.

"How's the wonderful world of doctoring?"

"Tiring today. I had surgery."

"Everything go okay?"

She nodded. "It had its moments, but he's fine."

Margo knew not to probe further. Grace rarely discussed

patients with any of her friends, determined to separate her work and personal life. She also learned from the few times she'd sought Margo's advice about a medical dilemma that she quickly became bored with the topic.

Instead, she bantered with Margo about the fashion choices of the patrons around them, only half listening as Margo listed the many reasons why Capris weren't really pants. It wasn't until she pulled a small wooden box from her purse that Grace looked up with complete interest.

"What's that?"

"This is an un-birthday present. Go ahead and open it."

She released the small metal clasp and stared at a vial filled with lavender liquid. She picked it up and studied it. "This is lovely, Margo. What's inside? It can't be food coloring, can it? I've never seen anything like this."

"Uh, no," Margo said, taking a sip of her martini. "It's something I picked up on my last trip to South America. It's a potion called Root of Passion. Whoever drinks it increases their passion and loses their inhibitions."

She laughed loudly. "You're kidding, right? You didn't *pay* for this did you?"

Margo stared at her seriously. "I did. I bought it for you, and I think you should drink a little."

Her jaw dropped. "Are you insane? Do you really think I'm going to ingest any foreign substance without knowing exactly where it came from? I'm a *doctor*."

"I know that, Grace, and I expected you to be skeptical—"

"And you're not? If you're so keen on this drink, why don't you try it?"

"Well, the last thing I need in my life is more passion, and, according to the woman who sold it to me, it wouldn't work on me. It has to be a gift."

"How convenient," she snorted. "No way."

She pushed the box away and motioned to the waiter. "Now, what I really want is another glass of merlot, one that is *approved* by the FDA."

Margo held the vial up in front of her. "Before you say no for good, I want you to study this like the scientist you are."

She shook it and the potion swirled inside, the lavender separating. Grace could see the individual red and blue colors. *Maybe you shouldn't have another glass of wine.*

"I'll admit that it's beautiful, but there's no way. Not gonna happen."

Margo sighed. Before Grace could stop her, she'd uncorked the vial and taken a sip.

"Are you crazy!" she bellowed, in a voice that drew the attention of many customers.

Margo licked her lips. "Not bad. It actually tastes like pineapple."

Grace studied her, watching her color, her eyes. If she went into shock or respiratory failure, Grace would need to perform CPR. Of course, if the potion was poison, then she was helpless. Even after the paramedics arrived, she wouldn't be able to tell them anything about the lavender liquid—its content, origin, even its scientific name.

"I can't believe you did that," she said, as Margo reached for her martini. Grace grabbed her wrist. "Do you really think you should be drinking? What if the potion and alcohol don't mix? What if the combination is toxic?"

Margo removed her fingers and sipped her drink. "Honey, I didn't notice any labels about avoiding alcohol or heavy machinery." She looked around the restaurant and grinned. "I feel fine. Just like the gorgeous saleslady promised. She said that it wouldn't have any effect on me. I guess she was right." She held up the vial. "Now, it's your turn. I've proven that there's nothing to be afraid of. Hell, Grace, it's probably a hoax. It's probably just water and some sort of coloring mixed together. What's the harm?"

She held up her hands, as if to push the vial away. "I'm not doing this, and I'm not having this discussion with you."

Margo sighed and returned the potion to her purse. "You need to, sweetie. You're in a holding pattern, and you need to spice up your life."

"Why? I'm completely happy. I'm a highly successful surgeon, who'll probably be a full partner in the practice within two years. I own my home, and if I do say so myself, I'm in pretty damn good shape."

Margo nodded. "All true. Which is why you are an incredible catch for a lucky woman. You just need to make yourself available."

"I *am* available. I date."

"When? Since Eva left, you've rarely been out to dinner." She took a deep breath and stared at her. "You're no fun."

"Ouch, Margo. That hurt."

"I'm sorry, but you need to know, and it's not just my opinion. Michelle agrees with me. But most of all, Eva agreed with me."

She wasn't surprised that Michelle, an old friend from high school, would hold that opinion but the mention of Eva reminded her of their previous conversation a few hours before.

"When did Eva say I wasn't any fun?"

Margo snorted into her martini. "Too many times to count. You were never there, honey. You weren't available, either physically or emotionally. It was all about work and getting ahead. Why do you think she broke up with you?"

She shrugged. She'd always suspected that Eva had been unfulfilled in the relationship, but neither of them really talked about the breakup. It had just happened—slowly—like a tire losing air. Eventually Eva just stopped calling, and she realized she was spending her Saturday nights alone.

"Why didn't you tell me this sooner?"

"Would it have mattered?"

"Probably not. My career is the most important thing in my life. It's—"

"The only thing in your life. Nothing else exists."

"That's not true," she said, but she knew her protest was weak. "I mean, I have friends, interests."

Margo pointed her olive at Grace. "Interests? You have a passing interest in art but you have no hobbies. Your friends tolerate you, honey, because we love you. Even when you ignore us, don't call, or cancel on us, we still love you. Eva thought she deserved more and she did."

"I thought you didn't know why she broke up with me."

Margo stared at her intently. "I lied. She told me you would never jump into life. You would never fully enjoy being with her. She couldn't deal with it. I'm sorry to tell you this." She clutched Grace's wrist and stared at her. "Hear me, sweetie. You've got to climb the rickety ladder up to the top of the tree of life. You can't be content with the fruit at arm's reach. The best stuff is up high."

She hung her head, disappointed and embarrassed that Margo had kept such a secret from her. She finished her wine in silence, no longer interested in dinner. Margo said nothing when she excused herself after draining her glass. She wanted to take a drive to clear her head, but the wine wrestled with her fatigue, and she found herself very sleepy. *All you need is a DUI, Gracie. That would spice up your life.*

She went home, drew a bath and poured a glass of merlot. As she settled into the tub, the swirling blue bath salts reminded her of the Root of Passion. There was no way she'd ever try it, but the idea of a potion that could free her from her anxiety was interesting. What if something like that could exist?

Fat chance.

Still, Margo's revelation about Eva cut deep. Why hadn't Eva told her? Was she that hopeless? Tears pooled in her eyes and she blinked them away. Love wasn't worth it. Romance was too hard, at least for her. She leaned back and closed her eyes, imagining the lavender separating in the vial.

Chapter Three

As was her custom, Grace allowed herself one extra hour of sleep on Saturday and Sunday mornings. It was a practical indulgence, but on this particular Saturday, when the buzzer sounded at eight, she could have easily ripped the alarm clock from the wall and stayed in bed indefinitely. Her body craved more rest, but she opened one eye and saw the glowing digital numbers flip from eight to eight-o-one. Another minute of her day—and her life—had passed, and she was still acting like a worthless slug. She commanded her other eye to open, taking another step toward commitment.

Her mind focused on the to-do list that hung on her refrigerator, a culmination of the week's epiphanies and necessary errands that demanded her attention: clean the bathroom, pay bills, write a thank-you note to Aunt Judith for the birthday gift—a book on modern art. She didn't bother drafting the note in her head, since it would come to her naturally. She loved art of all eras, but the modern period was one of her favorites. Then, too, there was work in the garden, and she owed her neighbors lunch for helping her fix the back gate.

She often tricked her body by reviewing her to-do list, and in ten minutes she was out the front door for her morning jog. It was a beautiful morning, and she loved running through her neighborhood, a stately pre-World War Two subdivision full of well-maintained cottages and bungalows. She turned the corner and saw Scott and Ray, her helpful neighbors, already out working on their yard.

"Come by for lunch," she called, stopping in front of their walk but continuing to run in place.

"We'd better have something good," Scott warned. He was clipping back some overgrown vines while his partner emptied the lawnmower bag. "None of that sickening seaweed stuff you gave us last time. There is a limit to healthy, Grace."

"You got it," she said, waving goodbye.

Why can't my yard look like that? She already knew the answer. When they weren't managing their interior design business, Scott and Ray trimmed, pruned and planted. She dismissed as a professional advantage the fact that the inside of their house looked equally fabulous.

She reached the end of the street, determined to run at least three more blocks before turning around, ignoring the cries of her thirty-six-year-old calves. She was starting to feel her age, and, as a doctor, she was wise to the changes that were coming. She knew she was prepared, having increased the fiber in her diet and abstaining from most fatty foods. Her only vice was red wine, but she rationalized that the health benefits counterbalanced the negative effects.

By the time she'd stumbled through her front door, her legs wobbled so badly that she fell on the couch, her confidence shaken, knowing she needed to increase her iron supplement. Her cell phone vibrated in her pocket. It was Margo. Unwilling to debate the Root of Passion anymore, she waited for the inevitable voice mail that she was certain Margo would leave and then replayed it.

"Hi, gorgeous. I'm sorry about last night. Look, I'm going to Rocky Point next month. Why don't you come along and keep me respectable? You need to start gambling, Grace, and I'm using that word metaphorically. The next time I go anywhere, you're coming with me, and I won't take no for an answer. And I still think you should try the Root of Passion."

There was a harsh click ending the call. She rolled her eyes and headed for the shower, determined to dismiss the message and forget Eva's comments. She couldn't change for anyone. Experience had taught her that whenever she took a risk, only hard lessons and regret were the result. She reasoned that people chose their misery by risking their fortunes unnecessarily, looking for shortcuts to bypass the true ingredients of lasting happiness: patience and hard work. And as a surgeon, she had an ample supply of both.

"Am I boring? Honestly."

Ray and Scott looked at her, both wearing confused expressions. Grace had lobbed the question at them without warning, hoping to gauge their honest reactions. Once the shock faded, they glanced at each other as if to decide who drew the short straw and would need to answer. After watching them shift in their chairs uncomfortably for another ten seconds, she didn't need a response—she'd already received it.

She sucked in her breath. "Okay, let me rephrase that question. Am I the most boring person you know?"

"No," Scott said quickly, and Ray slapped his shoulder. "What?" he snapped. "You disagree?"

Ray shook his head and offered her a gentle smile. "I don't think you're boring at all. You're just careful."

"Sounds the same," she said.

Scott speared a chunk of his Asian tofu salad. "Honey, I'm not sure where this whole conversation is going, but it doesn't bode well for our friendship. You've asked a loaded question, which you have decided is also rhetorical, and nothing Ray or I say will be right." He quickly chewed his bite and held up his fork to make another point. "This is just like that time when you asked us if we liked that non-returnable purple blouse. Remember?"

She remembered. She hadn't spoken to either of them for a week. She closed her eyes for a moment, realizing that she was lucky to have such wonderfully honest friends, ones who didn't speak in metaphors and who balanced out Margo.

"I'm sorry," she said. "Margo told me last night that Eva broke up with me because I wasn't any fun, and I should gamble more with my life. I guess I want to know if you both agree."

Ray shrugged and filled his plate with another helping of salad. "I'm not sure what she means. Should you take out your 401K and invest it in a strip club? Probably not."

She blanched at the thought. She was careful with her retirement plan, increasing her contributions based on a set schedule devised by her financial planner, who referred to her as the poster child for a healthy financial future.

"There are other ways to gamble," Scott said.

"Such as?"

"When was the last time you went to the store without a list?"

"It saves money if you know what you want," she argued.

Ray touched her arm. "What about just impulse spending? Just get what you want?" Her eyes narrowed at the foreign concept, and he shook his head. "Here's another one. What about just spending a Saturday afternoon doing *nothing*?"

Her eyes widened. "Nothing? But when would I get anything done?"

Scott sighed. "That's the point, honey. You just let the day take shape. No planning. It's exciting."

"Exactly," Ray agreed. "How many times have we called you to do something and you've refused because you had some mundane chore to complete?"

She had no answer. She knew she declined offers from all of

her friends more often than she accepted.

"When was the last time you got laid?" Scott asked pointedly.

She shook her head adamantly. "No way. I'm not gambling with sex. I'm a doctor."

He held up his hand in protest. "I wasn't suggesting you hit the bars. That was merely my poorly worded way of asking you if you'd had a date in the last six months."

"No, I've been busy with work."

Both of the guys bowed their heads at the overused cliché. Even she knew it was ridiculous. "I don't know why I avoid connecting with new people," she admitted.

Ray waved his fork at her. "What about that hot chick at the end of your block? Dina what's her name. Have you even spoken to her?"

Her cheeks burned and she looked away.

"I'm so disappointed," Scott chastised her. "We spent three hours counseling you about how to get to know that woman, and I can't believe you've ignored all that free advice." He looked at Ray and shrugged. "Why do we waste our time on her?"

"I don't think you'll *ever* meet her," Ray challenged.

"Okay, okay, I'm sorry," she said. "I'll make a point to introduce myself, but I can't imagine it going anywhere. She looks like she's eighteen."

"She's twenty-four," Scott said.

"Twenty-four? How do you know that?"

"Because *I* made the effort to meet her a few weeks ago when she was out walking her monstrosity of a dog."

"So?" she asked, recognizing that her punishment would be to pry each detail from Scott's memory.

"She didn't say a lot. She works for a landscaper, been in the valley for the last two years, and she's renting her house from the family who used to live there."

She shook her head. "Twenty-four?"

Ray touched her shoulder. "Honey, at this point for you, twenty-four is just right. Go out and have a good time. A *really* good time. You're not looking for a mate, just a date."

She sighed. "Fine. I'll go knock on her door. Will that make you both happy?"

They grinned and let the subject drop, regaling her with their plans for a hiking expedition to the Andes. She loved hearing about their vacations, which were never ordinary. While everyone she knew took cruises or tours through Europe, Ray and Scott traveled to unusual places and came back with the funniest vacation stories she'd ever heard. They'd gone on safari in Africa, hiked through Malaysia and spent time in Amsterdam's red-light district. As Ray reviewed the rigorous exercise routine they were using to prepare for their hike on the Inca Trail, it dawned on her that she'd surrounded herself with people who were nothing like her. Ray, Scott and Margo were her best friends, but she had nothing in common with them. *Why do they even like me?*

That question nagged at her long after they'd left. She wondered when they'd get sick of her and just give up on the lost cause that was her life. She glanced at her daily planner and busied herself with the other four things that needed to be done before Saturday ended. And indeed, by eight o'clock that night, she'd managed to reorganize her closet, clean the kitchen cabinets and write the thank-you note to Aunt Judith. She'd already decided that the rest of her evening would involve red wine, a hot bath and the mystery novel she'd picked up at the local women's bookstore, but not before she took out the garbage and recycling.

The street was typically quiet on Saturday nights since the area catered to working professionals. There were few families, but the children who lived on her block were well-mannered and helpful. It was ideal for her, and she couldn't imagine living anywhere else.

She glanced down the block at Dina Devereux's house, a small adobe that sat on the corner where the street dead-ended. Even her name was exotic, and it matched her lifestyle, or so Grace thought. She drove an antique, dark blue Ford truck, the kind with the tiny tailgate. Her front yard was a visual masterpiece. She often saw her outside on her hands and knees, planting and pulling weeds. She frequently wore cutoffs and tank tops, revealing a sinewy tanned body, including an interesting tattoo that sat at the base of her spine. Of course, Grace had never gotten close enough to examine it, but from a distance she could tell the artwork was intricate. They occasionally waved at each other whenever Dina drove by on her way into or out of the neighborhood. She had a great smile, and her HATE IS NOT A FAMILY VALUE bumper sticker clued Grace into her sexuality.

Dina's front light cast a warm glow over her porch. She was probably home, as the truck was in the driveway and lights were on inside. She wondered how Dina spent her nights. Often there were other cars parked along the curb, and she must have a multitude of friends who visited, but they were never loud or obnoxious.

She glanced once more at the little adobe house, thinking about her promise to Ray and Scott. She realized she'd forgotten to grab the mail and when she thumbed through it, she found something addressed to Dina. Judging from the return address it was probably junk, and she wouldn't even miss it if Grace tossed it into the trash, but Ray's challenge echoed in her ears.

I don't think you'll ever meet her.

She headed out the door, but her steps slowed the closer she came to the house, until she'd planted herself at the end of Dina's front walk. She tapped the letter in her hand, rationalizing that she really shouldn't bother her neighbor over such a triviality. She'd convinced herself to go home when the front door opened and Dina emerged, digging through her pockets for her keys. She was dressed as if she was hitting the clubs, in tight jeans, a black T-shirt and a faded denim jacket. Her short, brown hair fell in her eyes and she brushed it away with her hand. She didn't notice Grace until she headed down the porch steps.

"Oh, hi," she said, an electric smile on her face. "You live down the block, right?"

Now that Dina had pulled her into a conversation, Grace felt obligated to trek up the walk and introduce herself. *Why had she even bothered?* She automatically held out the letter.

"Um, I got some of your mail."

Still smiling, Dina shook her head. "Weird. I don't get how that mail lady makes these mistakes. I mean, it'd be one thing if we lived next door to each other, but she's totally confused. Last week I got this porno catalogue for some guy three streets down. I think she's pretty clueless."

Grace laughed in agreement. "I know. Sometimes I think we all should just meet in the middle of the street each evening to redistribute it."

"Now there's a plan. Oh, by the way, I'm Dina Devereux."

She stuck out her hand, and as Grace took it, she noticed she wore a different silver ring on each finger and several bracelets on her forearm.

"Grace Owens." She glanced at the truck and automatically stepped back. "Well, I can see that you were on your way out, so I'll let you get on with your evening. I just didn't want you to miss whatever exciting opportunity is mentioned in that letter."

Dina rolled her eyes. "I'm sure. Thanks for bringing it by."

Grace nodded and offered a feeble wave. *I've done what I promised to do. I met her. I even shook her hand. Ha.*

"Hey, Grace."

She whirled around. "Yes?"

"You wouldn't by any chance like jazz would you? I'm heading out to this great new club in Cave Creek that nobody knows is great yet. Do you wanna come?"

"Oh, no. I don't think so," she said automatically. "I've already got plans. But thanks."

Dina smiled. "Sure. I know it's totally short notice. Maybe next time."

Grace watched her hop into the truck, noticing she had a great figure. She quickly turned away and started back toward her house.

Dina pulled up beside her and called through the window, "Hey, let me know if you ever want to plant anything along the front. I could hook you up with some great shrubs."

"Thanks," Grace said, as Dina drove off.

She entered her quiet house and locked the front door, unsure of what she wanted. The idea of curling up in a hot tub seemed ridiculous now, and she couldn't talk herself into enjoying anything—a DVD, a project, not even a quick shopping trip on the Internet.

She lost an hour just meandering through the rooms, standing in the doorways, looking out the windows into the backyard and sitting at her dining room table. She replayed her conversation with Margo over and over, thinking of Eva and the little vial in the oak box. Each time she pushed the idea away as absurd, it eventually clouded her mind again.

Unable to stand the isolation of her house another minute, she went outside and stood in the center of her backyard, staring into the sky. An odd feeling overtook her, one she couldn't immediately name. And then it hit her.

Shit. This is loneliness.

Chapter Four

As she prepared to land in Paris, Margo sighed heavily. It had been a long flight.

It was always a long flight when she had to work with Norma Wilson.

Although Margo was a long-time employee with the airline, protocol demanded that the most senior flight attendant was called the first flight attendant on any trip. Traditionally, it was a position Margo held because most of the flight attendants were relatively new, but whenever she flew with Norma, who'd been hired a year before her, she was forced to hold her tongue and suffer Norma's petty abuses, which she hurled randomly at everyone who didn't sit in the cockpit.

During the ten hours they'd just spent in the air, Norma had berated Kacie for organizing the drink cart poorly, threatened to write up Trevor for snapping back at her and driven Valerie into the tiny lavatory for twenty minutes where she breathed into a paper bag to lower her blood pressure.

Although she criticized everyone, it seemed to Margo that Norma delighted in chastising her whenever they flew together, since she had an audience—all the flight attendants who liked Margo more and preferred her as the first flight attendant.

Margo also thought there was another reason Norma harbored ill-will against her: she was homophobic. She'd heard her make jokes about faggots and fag hags, and the two crosses she wore around her neck served as symbols of her devotion to the Baptist faith and obviously Leviticus. More than a few times, Margo had endured Norma's litanies on religion. What few knew was her glaring hypocrisy: Norma was a whore.

Staring at her as they taxied toward the gate, Margo scowled. Norma was a year older, forty-two, but her wholesome Midwestern upbringing—as she put it—preserved her beauty, and she could pass for thirty. Margo couldn't help but be a little jealous. She was dark-haired, while Norma was a blonde, and in their secret competition to bed the most customers, Norma was ahead of her by at least two dozen people—all of whom were men.

She couldn't understand how a devout Baptist could justify whoring around, but there was no way she'd ask. The explanation was most likely long and convoluted, and she figured that only God should be subjected to listening.

She glanced at her bag, stowed under the seat in front of her, and thought of the vial nestled in the oak box. After listening to Grace's adamant unwillingness to swallow the Root of Passion, she was having her own doubts. It had been different standing in the store with the goddess, Chayna. She'd been so sure, so willing to swallow the black liquid without a care. Grace was a doctor, though, and she spoke with such credibility and authority that Margo wondered if she'd behaved moronically.

She wasn't sure what to do. A part of her wanted to hurl the box into the Seine, but she was incredibly curious, and she couldn't get Chayna out of her head. She closed her eyes, and it was as if she was standing before her, smiling.

She whispered, "Yes, it is the right thing to do. You need to know that it works."

She quickly formulated a plan, but she wasn't sure she could go through with it.

"Margo, dear," Norma called, gaining her attention. "When the passengers debark, don't forget to smile. You didn't look very friendly on our last flight together."

Norma offered a winning smile and faced forward in her seat.

It was then she knew she could go through with it.

By the time the crew was settled into their hotel, it was nearly one a.m. That didn't stop the flight attendants from crowding into Norma and Margo's room to invade the mini-bar for snacks and liquor. If Norma had one redeeming quality, it was her willingness to pick up the tab. No one ever offered to help pay, and Margo imagined they saw it as compensation for enduring her abuse.

Within an hour they were pleasantly toasted and quickly vacated, having gotten what they came for—free alcohol. Only Margo remained, sipping her vodka tonic while Norma cracked open a tiny bottle of Dewar's.

"Crap, I need to clean out my glass and take a tinkle," she muttered.

She grabbed the water tumbler she'd used to slurp down a bad cabernet and headed for the sink. Margo saw her chance, and with only a sliver of regret, pulled the vial from the oak box that had traveled with her to France and carefully poured a few drops into the bottle. She heard the toilet flush and Norma emerged, waving the glass in front of her, urging her to pour the Dewar's.

She drained the alcohol and smacked the glass on the nearby dresser.

"Is it hot in here?" she asked, unbuttoning her blouse and discarding her bra.

Margo had seen her naked many times, as they frequently

shared a room, but her distasteful personality coupled with her Bible thumping beliefs kept Margo's libido in check. Now, though, Norma wasn't herself. She stared into the mirror, caressing her nipples and stroking her abdomen.

"I feel so incredible," she said. "It's like I'm on fire."

She faced Margo and unzipped her skirt, letting it fall to the floor, exposing her silver thong. Her hands continued to roam the contours of her body, eventually settling in her thick hair. She yanked the combs that secured her tight bun, and let her blond mane swirl about her face.

"What do you think? Should I wear my hair down more often?"

Margo stretched out on the bed, lacing her hands behind her head. She was definitely enjoying the show.

"I think you should dance for me."

Norma's eyes lit up, and she grinned broadly. She ran to the clock radio and surfed the FM band until she found Aerosmith singing *Walk this Way*. She jumped on the bed, hovered over Margo and gyrated to the music. Margo had never given Norma's perfect ass a second look. Of course, she'd never shaken it in her face before.

Norma danced like a stripper, flowing like a wave, and Margo wondered about her past careers prior to flight attendant school. Norma seemed oblivious to her presence, focused on the music and her own pleasure. She kept her eyes shut, letting her toned arms drift about, keeping her balanced on the bed.

"Take it off," Norma commanded. She stood directly over Margo, who reached up and peeled the silver thong away.

Aerosmith was replaced with The Moody Blues *Knights in White Satin*, and Norma swayed gently to the music, slowly spreading her legs apart.

"Like what you see, you big dyke?"

"I do." Margo sat up and stroked Norma's thighs until she moaned with pleasure. She hadn't swallowed any potion but she was definitely getting hot. "Does that feel good?"

Norma looked at her, pained and confused.

She wants it, but she's not supposed to want it.

"Yeah," she admitted. "It feels wonderful."

She gasped, and Margo could tell she was lightheaded and about to fall off the bed. She pulled her down and rolled on top of her. She quickly undressed, Norma's eyes never leaving her.

They lay together, and Margo settled her own mound against Norma's, finding a rhythm that matched the eerie strains of The Moody Blues classic. It didn't take long for Norma to climax, and Margo was quite surprised when a searing orgasm tore through her own body. She cried out, so loudly that she was certain Trevor heard her in the next room. She only allowed herself a second to analyze it. Perhaps it was Norma's beauty, the heat of the moment or the smug superiority that she felt in bedding her homophobic boss.

She smiled supremely, noted the look of bewilderment on Norma's face and trailed kisses down her stomach into the pot of gold.

Morning brought a pounding headache as the sun poured into the room. Margo sat up and the memories of the previous night clicked into place. Norma wasn't in the room, and in fact all of her things were gone. Suddenly thinking she'd overslept, Margo jerked her gaze to the alarm clock and was relieved to see she still had three hours before she was due to the airport.

She met the others for breakfast, and Trevor mentioned he'd seen Norma climbing into the airport shuttle an hour before. Kacie suggested she was meeting the pilot for a secret tryst, and they all laughed.

But Margo knew better, and a twinge of guilt pulled at her heart. Then she remembered her purpose and the way Norma always treated the flight crew, and her guilt evaporated like the creamer in her coffee.

The pre-flight meeting with the entire crew was clearly awkward for Norma, who made a point to stand between the captain and co-captain.

Does she need protection from me?

31

Norma's gaze remained on the captain's face throughout the meeting and for the first time that Margo could remember, Norma refrained from her usual chastising comments. She was silent, seemingly withdrawn and detached. An image of her gyrating on the bed filled Margo's head, and her body warmed at the thought.

It was good sex. No, she corrected herself, *it was great sex. And Norma wanted it. Over and over.*

"Teach me how to love a woman," she'd cooed in her ear.

Margo almost laughed out loud as the captain reviewed the flight information, remembering that Norma hadn't needed any training at all. She was a quick learner.

The meeting broke up and the crew dispersed to perform their pre-flight duties. Margo turned to go, but felt a hand on her elbow.

"We should probably talk," Norma whispered.

She led Margo into business class and they sat down. Norma faced her, looking pale, her lip trembling.

"I'm not sure how much you remember about last night. I mean, I thought I was drunk, so I was rather surprised when I woke up and I didn't have a hangover. And, I recall every detail of our little mistake."

Margo raised an eyebrow. "Mistake?"

"Of course it was a mistake," Norma hissed. "I'm not a dyke. I don't sleep with women."

The look of revulsion on Norma's face was a match that lit a fire inside of Margo. "Really? You seemed pretty into it last night. I've got your thong in my suitcase as a souvenir. Remember you said I should keep it?"

Margo stroked her hand until she yanked it away. There were tears in her eyes, as she obviously assessed the trouble that Margo could create for her.

"Margo, I'm not sure why it happened, but it won't happen again. I love Jesus, and I can't betray him with that kind of sinful behavior. I don't mean to put you down," she quickly added, "but I'm a God-fearing Christian, and we don't abide by your choices."

She hung her head. "As it is, I'm going to have to schedule a talk with my pastor and ask to be cleansed."

Margo pictured the good reverend pouring a gallon of bleach over her head.

"Norma, I promise I won't say anything to anyone, but I also think we shouldn't be on the same flights anymore."

She nodded vigorously. "I agree. If you see that I've signed up for a flight, you should just pick a different one."

As the senior flight attendant, Norma chose her schedule first, and of course she always picked the best flights at the best times. Margo's choice was to join her or pick the second-rate flights. She opted for a balance, ensuring that they only flew together half of the time.

"No," Margo said. "That's not going to happen. I'll keep my mouth shut, but from now on you'll let me pick first, and if I'm on a flight, you'll choose another."

Her jaw dropped. "That's blackmail."

"I know," she said. She kissed her cheek and gave her thigh a quick stroke. "But while I'm spiritual, I'm not a God-fearing Christian. And I won't hesitate to tack your little thong on the lounge bulletin board and never give a thought about how I'll pay in the afterlife."

Chapter Five

Mondays and Wednesdays were scheduled non-surgery days, and Grace enjoyed the change of pace. She volleyed between her office where she met new patients, and the hospital where she made rounds and checked on her post-op patients, like Chester Brown. The nursing staff spoke highly of him and said he always had a wealth of visitors.

It didn't surprise her to see half the family congregated around his bed when she tapped on the open door. They were laughing heartily at one of his stories, and Edna was seated next to him in the only chair the hospital provided.

"How ya doin', Doc?" he asked, scooping the last spoonful of Jell-O from a small plastic cup.

"I think that's my question," she said, smiling.

The various family members, all of whom looked like Chester,

Edna or a combination of the two, stepped back so she could examine him and check the surgical site. The room grew quiet as she listened to his heart.

"Everything seems to be going well for a day after surgery, so that's great."

"When does Grandpa get to go home?" a teenage boy asked.

"Probably not for at least a week. He needs to rest, and I really want to keep a close watch over him." She looked at Chester and patted his hand. "For a man of your age you came through remarkably well. You're in very good shape, too. What's your secret?"

He grinned and she realized he wasn't wearing his lower dentures. "It's my great life, Doc. I've been blessed with all of these wonderful children, grandchildren and a wife who always forgave me for my mistakes."

Edna shook her head. "You shush, Chet. There wasn't much to forgive. You've always been the best."

Her eyes welled with tears and she reached for a tissue.

"Don't you start blubbering, Edna," he said. "Anyway, thanks for everything, Doc."

"You're welcome. I'll let you all get back to your visit."

She returned to the nurse's station to update his file, and the family's chatter resumed. "Excuse me," a voice said.

Grace looked over her shoulder at an attractive woman. Her long blond hair was parted to one side and she was dressed casually in cargo shorts, a faded T-shirt and hiking boots. She carried a messenger bag instead of a purse, and she looked as if she'd stepped out of the woods. Grace immediately saw a resemblance to Edna.

"Hi, I'm Logan, Chester Brown's oldest daughter."

They shook hands, and Grace noticed the worry in her expression.

"He's doing well," she offered, and Logan's face immediately softened. "For a man of his age, he's making a remarkable recovery."

"Thank God. I don't know how my mom could live without him." She raked her hand through her thick hair and glanced toward his room. "I'm glad they're all here," she added, but made no effort to go inside.

She shuffled her feet and pulled at her bag, which bulged from the contents.

"I take it you've been away?" Grace asked.

She nodded. "I travel continuously for my job. I'm a freelance photographer, but I work mainly for *National Geographic*."

"That sounds interesting."

"It is. I wouldn't trade what I do for anything, but any time there's a family crisis I always feel like the odd woman out. I'm always the last one called and I'm not reliable like a typical oldest child." She sighed and glanced into the room again. "Well, I've taken up enough of your time. I'm sorry for dumping on you."

"Not a problem."

"Is there a timetable to get him out of here?"

Grace nodded. "He should stay for another week, just so we can keep an eye on him. We'll run some tests periodically, but he's doing great."

Logan touched her arm gently. "Yeah, my mom said there was a scary point in the surgery yesterday, but you pulled him through. I can't thank you enough."

"You're welcome."

Her hand slid away, but Grace's eyes remained glued to where the connection had occurred. *Geez, Grace. Has it been so long that any little touch turns you on?*

Logan joined her family, all of whom took turns embracing the long lost daughter returning from her travels. Grace could hear Chester laughing, and she imagined that he was quite proud of Logan.

Watching the family huddle together reminded her that she wasn't close to anyone. She'd been a surprise, born when her parents were in their early forties, long after they'd settled for one child, her brother, John, who was fifteen years older. Since their ultra-conservative views would never allow them to consider abortion, she'd been the obstacle that kept them from their early retirement, their endless days of tennis at the club and traveling the world. She visited them in Minneapolis twice a year, but it was always awkward. She and John maintained contact through Christmas card pleasantries, since he'd never accepted her lesbianism. *Who will care for you, Grace, should you ever get sick?*

"Hey, are you okay?"

She looked over at Eva, who stood at the nurse's station. "I'm fine. What are you doing on this floor?"

She held up a patient's chart. "Just covering for Tanya. She and her new boyfriend got stuck behind a tropical storm trying to get out of the Bahamas. They had to postpone their flight until tomorrow."

"Sounds potentially dangerous."

Eva scowled. "Only you would think that, Grace. The rest of the world would love to have another day of romantic bliss, stuck in a hotel, unable to hurry back to the doldrums of work."

She froze, stunned. "I'm not sure… what are you saying?"

Eva sighed and stared at the chart. "I'm not saying anything. Never mind." She started to walk away, but stopped and turned around. "Do you remember the trip we were planning the winter before we broke up?"

She automatically nodded, but she really didn't remember. Eva had handled all of the social activities. All she had to do was show up. She strained to replay the last year of their relationship, and then it dawned on her—they'd been planning their own trip to the Bahamas.

Chapter Six

As she gazed into her closet, Grace remembered Margo's comments about their dinner plans.

"We're going someplace nice," she said. "So, no pants and you'd better wear makeup."

"You're not fixing me up, are you?" she had asked suspiciously.

Margo cackled. "No, honey. I've learned my lesson on that front. This is just dinner. Simple and easy. You'll be home by ten."

Secretly she was disappointed that Margo clearly believed she was a lost cause. Still, Margo was her best friend and full of surprises. Maybe the evening would result in a potential date, and she allowed that sliver of optimism to guide her fashion choices. She picked a sleek black dress, which was definitely the sexiest thing she owned. She'd bought it on a whim when Margo had taken her shopping one afternoon after they'd consumed more liquid than solids at lunch. Margo knew alcohol was her Achilles' heel and had taken full advantage of her when they wandered into Macy's dress department. The hemline came well above her knees, and two ribbons of black silk trailed up her chest, barely covering her breasts, and fastened behind her neck. *For such an expensive dress, there isn't much material above your waist, Gracie.* What would her patients think if they happened to see her out in public? And what would Eva think?

She resisted the urge to change into a conservative blouse and skirt, and, to confirm her commitment to her sexy look, she removed the clips that secured her hair and shook her blond mane as it tumbled over her shoulders. She smiled slightly. She *looked* ready for action even if she had no intention of acting upon anything. She touched up her red lipstick, pleased with the result. She'd never thought of herself as vain, and others said she was pretty, even if she spent most of her life hiding it underneath a long white coat and sensible shoes.

When Margo appeared on her doorstep twenty minutes later, she applauded. "Surgeon by day, sizzling sexpot by night. Let's go see how many heads you can turn."

As they headed for Margo's idling Mustang, Grace savored her effusive praise. She reached for the passenger door handle and glanced down the sidewalk at a white blur bounding toward her. She remained frozen in place, too surprised and too slow to move out of its path—whatever *it* was.

As if stepping into a spotlight, the streetlight caught its form for a split-second, long enough for her to realize that Pepper, Dina Devereaux's Harlequin Great Dane, was charging her. His tongue flapped from side to side, and she estimated she'd be flattened momentarily.

"Cease!" a voice commanded.

Pepper's paws immediately tangled as he attempted to obey. Instead of toppling Grace, he merely collided into her legs, but the force of one hundred and thirty pounds while she tried to stay balanced in two-inch heels was too much. She dropped to the ground, albeit gently. Pepper sat in front of her panting.

Dina finally caught up to her dog and Grace. "Are you okay?" she asked anxiously, extending her hand.

"I think so."

She rose and quickly adjusted the top of her dress, which had slipped to one side, revealing most of her left breast. Her gaze shot to Dina's face.

She raised her eyes from Grace's overexposed chest, her cheeks crimson. "Um, I'm really sorry about Pepper. He saw Mrs. Reemer's cat just a few seconds ago, and he took off. Then he saw you, and he hates to see people leave. I'm so sorry. Are you sure you're okay?"

"I'm fine," she said, suddenly realizing that Margo had remained inside the Mustang during the whole ordeal. *She's probably on her cell phone.*

"Well, you look absolutely amazing." Dina nodded toward the Mustang. "Are you going on a date?"

"Oh, no. I'm just going to dinner with my friend. We're just friends," she said again, feeling like a complete idiot.

Dina's eyes slid away from her face and down her body— slowly. She seemed to savor each curve covered by the black silk. When their eyes finally met again, she offered no apologies for her forward behavior, but instead stepped toward Grace and touched her shoulder.

"I hope you have a wonderful evening," she whispered. "And you look incredible."

She turned away and Pepper immediately followed, trotting next to his mistress, who sauntered back down the street, her hands stuffed inside her front pockets.

Grace took a deep breath, trying to calm her racing heart, and joined Margo inside the Mustang. Thelonius Monk's trademark jazz floated through the car and Margo's head rested against the leather seat, her eyes closed.

Her eyes still closed, Margo inquired, "Are you ready to go now, or should I just drop you off at the end of the cul-de-sac for a quickie?"

"Margo!" Grace feigned indignation. "I hardly know Dina."

A wicked smile crossed her face. "Honey, you practically exposed yourself. I guarantee that if you went and knocked on her door right now, she'd whip that dress off you in about two seconds."

"I seriously doubt that," she disagreed weakly. "Can we go now, please? I'm starving."

She desperately needed Margo to charge out of the neighborhood, away from Dina.

Margo put her hand on the gearshift and looked over at her. "Last chance. I can just as easily knock this baby into reverse and coast down your street all the way to her front door."

She stared ahead. "Unbelievable."

Margo leaned over the seat and put her arm around her. "I dare you to let me back this car right into her driveway. I dare you to knock on her door and let her see *both* your tits."

She scowled. "You *dare* me? How old are we? Nine? Are you going to double-dog dare me next?"

"No, first, I'd have to double-dare you." Margo sighed heavily and put the car into drive. "Life's passing you by, sweetie."

As if to make a point, she floored the gas. Grace lurched backward in her seat, and the car screeched down the quiet street, instantly distancing her from the temptation that was Dina and dissolving another opportunity for her to change her life.

The encounter with Dina bothered her throughout dinner. She continually replayed the lustful look on Dina's face when she'd fallen to the ground, and the incredible eyes that couldn't turn away from her own. Margo didn't notice and conversed enough for both of them, and as long as Grace asked questions occasionally and continued to nod in the appropriate places while she sipped her merlot, she could let her mind wander deeper into her private thoughts.

"So have you reconsidered accepting my generous present?" Margo asked, sipping her after-dinner brandy.

She raised an eyebrow. "If you're asking am I ready to imbibe some unknown liquid, no, I'm not. I won't be snorting any cocaine either."

"Fine. But you might be interested in a piece of gossip I picked up the other night at Destiny's."

She knew Destiny's far too well. Eva had insisted they go to Happy Hour at least twice a week, and while the house merlot was decent, Grace had spent most of the evenings watching Eva flirt with other women.

"What?"

"I was at a table with Naomi, one of the lesbian flight attendants I like to party with, and I overheard these three women talking. I didn't turn around, but above all of the music I recognized one of the voices. This woman with the familiar voice kept talking about how much she missed her lover. She'd dated all of these other women, but no one compared to the *doctor* she used to date."

Grace's heart beat faster. "Did you see who it was?"

Margo smiled. "Of course. And I think you can guess."

"Did she see you?"

"No. She was too involved in her conversation and she was pretty toasted. So, the news for you, Gracie, is that your ex is still pining for you. You actually might have another chance with her, if you want it. But you definitely would need to make more of an effort."

As Grace shook her head, Margo was already pulling the oak box from her purse.

"No way, Margo. Besides, if Eva wants me back, she needs to be content with the real me."

"You're not even content with the real you."

She stood and grabbed her purse. "I'm not discussing this any further. I've got to hit the bathroom."

She meandered through the restaurant, unable to believe that Margo wanted her to swallow the potion. And she couldn't believe Margo had tried it. She'd handled dozens of poisoning cases during her ER rotation as a resident, and some of them were gut-wrenching. She pictured Margo laid out on a gurney, her lips lavender.

When she returned, Margo was flipping her cell phone shut. "That was Joseph. I hope you don't mind, but I invited him and Michelle to join us. They're right around the corner at that little Irish bar."

"Sure," she said, with little enthusiasm. "The more the merrier." A fresh glass of merlot had arrived while she was gone, and she drank greedily. She loved Joseph, a chemist who worked at the hospital, but anytime she faced Michelle she needed a little buzz.

She took another swallow, feeling lightheaded. "Are you hot?"

Margo shook her head, staring at the table. "No, in fact I think they've got the A.C. on too low. I'm starting to get chilly." Margo wouldn't meet her gaze. She narrowed her eyes. Something was up. "Margo, what's going on?"

Margo glanced up for a second. "Sometimes, Grace, I just need to help you."

"What are you talking about?"

Her eyes drifted to the vial that rested in the box on the table. Suddenly she realized more of the Root of Passion was missing. She held up the almost empty wineglass.

"You didn't."

Margo placed her hand over Grace's. "Now, don't panic. I just put a few drops in your wine. Take a deep breath."

"How can I *not* panic? You may have poisoned me! Right now my entire nervous system—"

"Breathe. Just once. Take one deep breath for me."

Realizing that Margo wouldn't allow the conversation to continue until she'd followed her instruction, Grace closed her eyes and took a deep breath—and was calm. She opened her eyes and leaned back against the booth's leather headrest. She checked her pulse. Normal. She still felt incredibly warm, and when she cradled herself into the leather booth, every nerve seemed to react. An image of Alice sliding down the rabbit hole flashed through her mind, but she let it go. She let it all go. It was as if her entire body deflated, and she was nothing but a malleable piece of clay.

"Are you okay?"

She nodded and a slow smile crept over her face. She couldn't believe what was happening. A burst of energy surged through her, one that was impossible for her medical mind to decipher. She didn't feel high or stoned—just refreshed. The pebble of doubt that lived in the corner of her mind was dislodged, and when she scanned the couture of the women sitting at the nearby tables, she made a firm conclusion.

"I look damn good, don't I?" she asked Margo.

"I think it's working," she said blandly. "There's Joseph and Michelle."

Margo quickly closed the small box and shoved it in Grace's purse. She waved toward a dapper black man in jeans and a dress shirt, and a woman in tight leather pants and a silk blouse with so much lace that Grace wondered if it was really a negligee top from the lingerie department.

"Hey ladies," Joseph said as he slid next to Margo in their semi-circular booth.

Michelle sat beside her and smiled sexily. "How are you, Grace?"

"I'm fine," she said, her body temperature rising again.

That seemed to happen whenever she and Michelle shared airspace. Michelle was a former model turned concierge at the Scottsdale Fairmount. They had known each other since high school and had dated briefly until Michelle discovered a French foreign exchange student who was willing to teach her more than vocabulary.

Somehow they remained friends, and while Grace spent years studying and toiling to achieve her career goals, Michelle had wandered aimlessly from job to job, her incredible looks conveniently opening doors for her. She wasn't motivated to find a real career, content to work from eight to five at any job that could support her love of expensive shoes.

"I've missed you," Michelle whispered, patting her thigh. "You look totally hot."

"Thanks," she said, dismissing the flirtation as overt friendliness.

That was how they talked to each other. Still, she was a little surprised when Michelle didn't remove her hand and began stroking her thigh. Grace was now certain that the air conditioning was broken or she was having a premature hot flash. Joseph listened as Margo recounted her trip to South America, both of them entirely ignoring Michelle and Grace. It was inevitable when the four of them got together, but Grace suddenly wished they could find a mutual topic of interest, anything to distract Michelle from what clearly seemed to be her mission for the evening—help Grace have an orgasm in public.

"What are you doing?" she hissed.

Before Michelle could answer, the waiter brought Grace another glass of merlot, flashing a creepy grin in her direction. Joseph ordered a bottle of Pinot Noir and a vodka tonic for Michelle.

"That must be some merlot."

"Why would you say that?" Grace asked.

"It would definitely explain the expression on your face, and your rather sexually explicit pose."

She immediately sat straight up and frowned. "What are you talking about?"

"Now, why did you do that? I and probably many of the restaurant patrons were enjoying a lovely view of your cleavage, particularly your right breast."

What the hell is going on with my breasts tonight? I might as well have gone topless.

She was mortified. She tapped Margo on the shoulder and waited for Joseph to finish an anecdote about his experience with speed dating.

"Why didn't you tell me I was exposing myself to everybody in the restaurant?"

Michelle snorted. "Geez, Grace, get over it. It's no big deal. It's like when you see some woman come out of a bathroom and her skirt's still stuck in her slip."

"Or when a guy forgets to zip up his fly," Joseph said.

Margo clapped her hands together and started to laugh. "I was in the mall one time and this little kid was with his mother and this gang banger, who I'm guessing was the father. Anyway, the guy's pants are sagging to his knees, and the little kid comes up behind him and grabs his pants to get his attention, and he pulls them all the way down." Everyone started to laugh, but Margo waved her hand. "That wasn't the best part. The guy was so surprised and disoriented trying to catch the kid that he tripped. He looked like some sort of insect, lying on his back trying to get his pants pulled up. It was the funniest thing I've ever seen!"

They were all laughing so hard that at first Grace didn't feel Michelle's hand stroking the side of her breast. Once she did, she turned and faced her. Michelle parted her gorgeous lips, both carefully lined and shaded in a rich pink hue.

"Oh, baby," she whispered, as her fingers brushed against Grace's nipple. Because Michelle had angled her body sideways, none of the other patrons noticed, and Joseph and Margo were slugging back glass after glass of Pinot as if they'd entered a contest.

Grace should have moved away, or at least removed Michelle's hand, but the touch resounded through her body, and she imagined the Root of Passion coursing through her system.

Instead, she inched closer to Michelle, who whispered, "We're going home together. No arguments, doctor."

When they'd finished their drinks, Grace announced Michelle would give her a ride, and Margo and Joseph looked stunned. Then Margo smiled knowingly and glanced at her bulging purse that held the oak box.

They'd barely made it through the door before Michelle unfastened the ribbons of silk and cupped her breasts lovingly.

"It's about time we just took this off," she said, reaching for the zipper and letting gravity do the rest. All that remained were her lacy underpants, which she knew were soaked from Michelle's endless foreplay in the restaurant.

She gasped when Michelle forcefully knocked her onto the couch. The room spun, and she became slightly disoriented.

"What'd you do that for?" She attempted to rise but found her equilibrium wouldn't cooperate. It was as if the bones in her body had disappeared.

She looked up, watching Michelle discard the lacy blouse and slip out of her leather pants.

"Now," Michelle said, still hovering over her, "How drunk are you? Are you hung over?"

She shook her head slightly, entranced by Michelle's incredible body and a mole that sat slightly above her left breast. "I'm not drunk. I don't have a headache and I don't feel sick. My pulse and heart rate are steady. I'm just totally relaxed, and it's like I swallowed a bottle of muscle relaxants."

"You sound just like a doctor," Michelle slurred.

"I am a doctor."

"Well, Dr. Owens, we're going to play a little game. Perhaps you know it? It's *called* Doctor."

They indeed played quite a game, until Grace led her to bed and proved that medical school had taught her more about female genitalia than any lesbian sex book ever could.

When Grace opened her eyes the next morning, she was keenly aware of the light snoring next to her, and the cascade of melon-scented reddish-brown hair that rested against her cheek. She kissed Michelle's cheek and she stirred.

"Oh, God. What happened? It feels like a bull is standing on my head. How much did I drink?"

"You had four vodka tonics."

"Well, you had more than me, and you're not hung over?"

"No," Grace said, unwilling to share anything about the Root of Passion. "It's probably my metabolism."

Michelle sat up on one elbow, her eyes barely open, shaking her head. "I have no idea what you're talking about, Doc." She lifted up the sheets and glanced at their completely naked bodies.

"And I'm assuming we rekindled our flame from high school last night."

Grace's jaw dropped. "You don't remember the sex? You don't remember the way you ordered me to play with myself until I was about to orgasm?"

Michelle's face screwed up into disgust. "I did *what*? That's not my game. Hell, I don't play games. Straight sex."

"Not last night. You were like a dominatrix."

"What? Now I know you're full of shit. You must have been totally trashed and you're making up stuff." She pulled the covers off and began searching for her clothes.

"They're in the living room. That's where we started," Grace said, pointing to the door.

Michelle left and came back a few seconds later, holding her own clothes and Grace's dress. "Now, I *do* remember this dress."

"Do you remember how you got it off me?"

Michelle shook her head. "Not a clue." She glanced about the room and saw Grace's vibrator on the nightstand. "Okay, so if you remember everything, what did we do with that?"

Grace smiled timidly. "After the third time, you insisted I get it out."

"No, I never use a vibrator, not since—"

"Not since the French foreign exchange student forgot to lube it before she used it on you during high school."

Michelle looked horrified. She sat on the bed and hung her head. "I told you that story? I've never told anyone about that."

Grace reached over and stroked her beautiful back. "Sweetie, it's okay. Besides, you certainly enjoyed it last night. Of course, you insisted on taking my lube home with you. Proclaimed it as a miracle cure."

Michelle shot her a stabbing glare. "No way."

She pointed to her purse, and Michelle began fishing through it. When she pulled out a half empty tube of lubricant, she started to laugh. "This is un-fucking believable! You're telling me that I did some dominatrix thing with you in the living room, and then I changed into some vibrator-happy lush who fell in love with a tube of lube?"

Grace paused, thinking of a way to explain. The change in Michelle had been noticeable, and as a doctor she had been fascinated by the gradual crumbling of her calm exterior as the alcohol seemed to affect her more and more as the night wore on, until her speech was incoherent and she began singing old Dusty Springfield tunes—a tidbit Grace decided not to share.

"It was an interesting night," Grace said. "One that we probably shouldn't repeat. As a physician, I'm advising you to stay away from vodka tonics. I think they're a little strong for you."

Michelle started putting on her clothes and turned away. "I'm too embarrassed to talk about this anymore, Grace. I'm just going to go."

Grace sensed the awkwardness of the moment and headed for the bathroom. "I think I'll take a shower."

Michelle said nothing as she shut the door between them. Why was last night so clear to her? It had been one of the greatest sexual experiences of her life. She'd craved Michelle's touch, and she was thrilled when she brought Michelle to orgasm. Granted, she felt tired and she decided to skip her morning run, but there was no hangover. She'd been in fabulous control the whole time. *Did the Root of Passion actually do that?*

When she finally came out of the bathroom after a long, hot shower, Michelle was gone. She got dressed and went into the kitchen to make coffee. On the counter, she found a note in Michelle's perfect script, the lube next to it.

Grace,

I'm speechless about last night. I'm glad we had a great time, but I'm so sorry that I can't remember it. The fact that you can—the fact that you even _let_ me seduce you, and best of all, the fact that you aren't totally wasted is incredibly significant.

I'm making a list of everything you should do with your life. You know how much I love you, so here it is:

1.Face a fear and overcome it.

2.Have sex with a stranger.

3.Make a public spectacle of yourself.
4.Alter your appearance for sex appeal.
5.Have a relationship!

If you're wondering where I got this list, I called Margo and we made it together. Actually, we made it a long time ago, one night after we'd finished an entire bottle of Pinot Noir and were psychoanalyzing you. You're a great topic of conversation, honey. Change your life, sweetie!

P.S. Despite what I may have told you last night, I don't need this lube. I have more than you'll ever own.

Chapter Seven

The late Friday afternoon brought a flurry of activity when the nurse's shift change occurred. Grace tuned out the buzzing dialogue that surrounded her, focusing on her patients' charts. She reached for Chester Brown's thick notebook and smiled. She prided herself on a positive bedside manner and a devotion to listening to all of her patients, but she had to admit that she had her favorites and he was one of them. Inevitably he had visitors—his children, friends or former co-workers who taught with him at Trevor Browne High School. She learned that he'd spent nearly thirty years teaching biology and anatomy, and her personal bias toward science contributed to her affinity for the old codger.

When she knocked on his door today, Logan stood by the nightstand propping up some photos.

"Come in, Doc," he said with a wave. "Let me show you something."

He pointed to a five by seven photograph—a picture of him with Edna, leaning against a stone wall.

Grace looked closer and saw the extensive path. "Is that the Great Wall of China?"

"Yep. The kids gave us a trip to China for our fortieth wedding anniversary. We had a blast. It was almost as much fun as skiing in Switzerland."

"Wow, it sounds like you guys have really gotten around."

He shrugged. "We've been lucky. Edna had a good job selling real estate, and we were careful." He playfully grinned at Logan before he added, "And lucky for us, none of our kids gave us any real grief. We never had to bail one out of jail. None of 'em was a drug addict who stole from us. Just great kids."

"We were perfect," Logan summarized.

"Well, I wouldn't go that far." He pointed at her. "Especially you, missy. You gave your mother heart failure on more than a few occasions. You see, Dr. Owens, Logan takes after her old man. She's always had a bit of the wanderlust, always pushed the limits. Wanted skydiving lessons at sixteen, trekked through Europe after high school graduation—"

"And before he says it, I'm the only one who never went to college."

He sighed dramatically and placed his hand over his heart. "Yes, that nearly killed me. Imagine, Dr. Owens, a teacher's daughter *not* pursuing higher education."

"No, I pursued my passion instead," Logan said.

He reached over and squeezed her hand. "Yes, you did. You became a famous photographer and proved me wrong in the process. I was happy to let you tell me that you told me so."

He turned back to Grace and pointed at a row of pictures that lined the window. The room had gradually filled with more framed photos, some of the family, but many of exotic places that looked majestic and beautiful.

"Logan took every single one of them. She's been everywhere, met kings and queens, and she's even photographed celebrities. Matter of fact, she's shooting a wedding for Kazmar Edens and that model girlfriend of his this weekend in Vegas."

"Really?" Grace was impressed.

While she didn't follow celebrity gossip, it was inescapable when she was standing in the grocery store checkout line. Kazmar's handsome face stared at her from at least three different magazine covers each week. And now that he was getting married after only dating a Brazilian model for two months, the paparazzi and the tabloids were having a field day.

Logan shrugged. "It's not a big deal, really. He's a cool guy. We hit it off pretty well when I did his *GQ* shoot last year, and I already knew his bride, Lena."

"I thought you worked for *National Geographic*?"

"They just buy most of my stuff because it's of nature or places. I don't snap a lot of people."

"I see. Well, I imagine it will be an incredible affair."

She smiled at Logan, who offered a hard stare. She felt as though she was being studied, like one of her photography subjects. She looked away, momentarily flustered. When she absently touched her stethoscope, she remembered why she was there. "Okay, let's take a listen."

She checked his heart, examined his incision and took his vitals. She wasn't aware that Logan was snapping pictures of her until she stepped to the other side of the bed. When she looked up, Logan lowered the camera from her face.

"Sorry. Force of habit. Are you okay with this or should I stop?"

Never one to enjoy being photographed, Grace was slightly annoyed by the enormous lens focused on her, but she nodded anyway. She wore a striking plum blouse and perhaps Logan found it quite photogenic. She couldn't imagine any other reason why a world famous photographer would want to take pictures of her.

Logan held the camera with strong, confident hands, and her

casual body posture conveyed her ease with her art. She looked—sexy. That was it. Grace couldn't imagine a stethoscope adding to her sex appeal in the same way, but Logan seemed mysterious and incredibly interesting. For a split second, a textbook image of the central nervous system flashed in her mind, the lavender potion traveling through her bloodstream.

"Don't worry about it, Doc," Chester said. "She doesn't mean anything by it. She just can't help herself. She takes pictures of everything. It's not like she's going to plaster 'em all over the Internet. I can't tell you how many pictures she's taken of me."

"Too many," Logan murmured as she moved to the foot of the bed. "You've cost me thousands. Your ugly mug broke two of my lenses."

He laughed heartily and Grace chuckled. "Well, you seem to be doing well, improving slowly. Are you having any pain I should know about?"

He shook his head. "Nope, I'm feeling great. I'm hardly taking any pain meds now, too. Any chance I can get out of this joint pretty soon? The world's passing me by."

She smiled. *Interesting choice of words.* "I'm glad you're feeling better, but I can't let you go until I'm sure you're stable. I'm hoping for Monday." She patted his arm. "Dr. Van Buren will be by over the weekend to check on you, but if there's a problem he'll page me."

She nodded at Logan and headed out of the room, grateful to be away from her and her camera. She was getting an entirely different feeling about her today, one that was completely unprofessional. She found an open carrel outside the nurse's station and updated her notes in Chester's file.

"Dr. Owens?"

She glanced up at Logan, leaning against the wall, her arm draped over the carrel. Logan wore several bracelets made of leather and woven cloth, and Grace imagined they were trinkets collected during her many travels. A clenched fist dangled from her arm, and she pointed at it.

"What's that?"

"A figa. It originally was a symbol of oppression during the eighteenth century but it evolved into a good luck charm—but only if it's a gift from one person to another."

Just like the Root of Passion.

"I assume someone special gave you that?"

Logan rested her chin in her palm and grinned mysteriously. "There's a story there. A very beautiful woman, a week stuck in the sweltering desert and some incredible nights."

"Ah." An image of Logan naked flashed through her mind, and she cleared her throat to erase it. She set her pen down and folded her hands together, determined to keep a professional distance. "Is there another question I can answer for you?"

"Actually there are several. First, may I call you Grace?"

"I suppose."

"Now, Grace, I got this feeling when we were in my dad's room that there was some chemistry between us. Did you feel it?"

Her forthright nature smacked Grace in the face. "What?"

"I'm not getting this wrong, am I?" she whispered. "We've been checking each other out like crazy, so I assumed…" She didn't finish the thought, but when Grace said nothing, she stood up straight and shook her head. "I'm sorry."

She sauntered away, and Grace focused on her tanned, muscular calves. Suddenly Logan whirled around and faced her. "Gotcha."

Two nurses standing nearby glanced in her direction momentarily. There was no hiding her embarrassment. She touched her burning cheeks, certain they were crimson.

"Okay," Logan said, returning to the carrel. "You've indirectly answered both of those questions, so now I've got one more."

"What?" Grace asked, staring at her pen.

"I was told specifically by Kazmar that I could bring someone to his wedding. Would you like to come with me?"

Grace stiffened. "What?"

"Is that all you can say? You seemed far more erudite with my dad."

Grace clenched her pen tightly and carefully chose her words. "It's just that I make it a rule to separate my personal and professional life. This is not an appropriate conversation to have in the hospital."

"So, if I wait until you walk to your car and call you on your cell, then can we talk?"

There was no mistaking the suggestiveness of Logan's voice. And Grace couldn't decide if she liked it.

"Do you always invite complete strangers on trips?"

Logan laughed. "It's only for two days. Basically fly in and fly out. It's not like I'm kidnapping you for weeks."

Before temptation took control of her mouth, she said, "Um, well, thank you. It's just, this is such short notice, and frankly, your request is rather unorthodox. We hardly know each other, Logan."

"But you're feeling that connection between us, aren't you?"

She knew it was pointless to lie. She was a terrible liar, and Margo insisted it was the main reason she was still alone.

"I'll admit that I think you're very attractive. But why me?"

Logan leaned closer and whispered, "Because I'm guessing that underneath that starched white coat are an incredible body and a wild personality."

How wrong you are. She shook her head. "Thanks, but the answer's no."

Logan pulled out a slip of paper from one of the pockets in her vest, plucked Grace's pen from her hand and wrote down her phone number.

"In case you change your mind. I'm leaving tonight at nine. Now, I'm going to walk out of here for real this time and you have my permission to stare at my legs or my ass—whatever it was you were looking at before. I promise not to embarrass you again."

Grace couldn't resist watching Logan's confident swagger and sumptuous legs as she headed down the hallway. She was incredibly flattered by the invitation, but of course she'd never accept it.

She finished the notes and headed downstairs to change. She was meeting Margo for drinks, and she vowed not to mention the proposition or Margo would never stop talking about it, insisting she call.

She was so focused on her thoughts that she practically ran into Eva as she turned a corner. "God, I'm sorry."

"It's okay," Eva said. A moment of awkwardness passed as it always did when they weren't surrounded by twenty other people, and she added, "Are you leaving?"

"Yeah, I'm ready for the weekend."

Eva seemed to process this information like a difficult math equation. She bit her lip and leaned against the wall. "Got any big plans?"

"Oh, nothing much, really."

Eva chuckled. "Of course not. I forgot who I was talking to."

"Excuse me?"

"Nothing," Eva said quickly. "I just know that your weekends usually have a very strict blueprint."

"A blueprint?"

"Well, it's just that you're a planner and you don't like a lot of surprises. You want everything to be crossed off your to-do list. That's all I meant."

She started to fume. She was tired of Eva's mocking tone. "Well, not that it's your business, but I was invited to Kazmar Edens' wedding and I'm still deciding whether or not I should attend. What's your opinion, Eva? Should I forego my sacred to-do list for this once-in-a-lifetime opportunity?"

Instead of answering, Eva's jaw dropped, and Grace savored the moment of total surprise as she walked away.

Chapter Eight

"Let me make sure I understand. You, Grace Owens, have been invited to attend the hottest wedding of the year, which happens to be the most sought after publicity event in recent history, and you said *no*."

She hadn't meant to tell Margo, but it had just slipped out as she recounted the meeting with Eva and her sarcastic response. They were sitting at the Monastery enjoying Happy Hour, and Grace had already finished her second merlot.

"I can't believe you guys made that list," she said, hoping to change the subject.

Margo pointed at her. "This is exactly what the list is about. Give it to me. I know you have it with you."

She scowled and searched her purse until she found the sheet of memo paper.

I should have burned it. Instead I've reviewed it at least a dozen times.

"Do you really think I'd have sex with a stranger?"

Margo lifted her glass. "Honey, you slept with Michelle after nearly twenty years. Anything's possible." She took her hand and looked at her with sincerity. "I love you, sweetie, but Michelle's right. You've got to loosen up, and I think you're passing up an incredible chance. Call Logan. Tell her you'll go. Kazmar Edens is the hottest actor on the planet. And you still have the rest of that vial," she added.

She absently touched her bulging purse. The small oak box was buried near the bottom. She'd meant to take it out but had conveniently forgotten. "I'm not drinking anymore of that potion," she said weakly, shifting her purse away from Margo.

When another mutual friend, Celeste, stopped by their table, Grace couldn't find an appropriate moment to leave. Margo ordered another round and told Celeste about Grace's missed opportunity.

"I can't believe you're not going if for no other reason than to see the art collection," Celeste said.

"What do you mean?" Grace asked. She adored art and visiting museums, but she hadn't been to one in ages, not since Eva had left. It was one of the activities they both relished.

"Well, I heard that Kazmar was getting married at Linus McWhirter's estate. And he's known for his art collection. His mansion is unbelievable. It was featured once on *Lifestyles of the Rich and Famous*. He's got an original Degas, a Kahlo, and a Richter, among others. Considering how much you love paintings, Gracie, I'm surprised you're not jumping at the chance."

Margo sighed deeply. "But unfortunately, Celeste, Grace would have to endure the tedious company of a beautiful and talented photographer, who's made it very clear that she wants to make time with the good doctor."

Celeste touched her breast dramatically. "How horrible!"

Grace quickly excused herself and went to the bathroom. She didn't know what to do. Since her evening with Michelle she kept seeing herself standing on a hill, looking down at a tiny town. It was sleepy, ordinary. She felt pity for everyone who lived there, stuck in their ho-hum lives, while she towered above them, close to the clouds, free. She knew it was symbolic and stupid at the same time. Still, it was as though she'd inherited an incredible power, over herself and others. She savored the feeling.

Her cell phone rang, and she was surprised to see Eva's name. She'd never bothered to remove her from her address book. *Was that significant?*

"Hey," she said.

"Hi, Grace." Her voice sounded shaky, hesitant, not at all like the usually jovial Eva who was the life of the party. "Um, I wanted to apologize for the comments I made earlier. I had no right to speak to you like that. I'm sorry."

She slurred her words and music played in the background. Grace asked, "Are you drunk?"

Eva chuckled. "Only a little. And don't worry. I'm not driving."

"Where are you?"

"At Destiny's. I'm just checking out the hot women."

"So, who's taking you home?" she asked playfully.

"Shit, Grace. I'm not some whore."

Confused, she sputtered, "Eva, I wasn't implying—"

"Sure you weren't. When we were together, you resented all the women who wanted me."

"I did not."

"You sure the hell did. That's why you hated coming here."

Grace looked around the bathroom and sighed. She didn't want to have a phone argument in the middle of the restaurant's facilities. "Eva, you're drunk. I'm hanging up now."

"That's just like you, Gracie. Run away from a conversation. Have fun with your great celebrity weekend."

"Goodbye, Eva. And in case you're wondering I accept your apology, but I think you owe me another one."

She shut the cell phone and stood over the sink. Eva would immediately retreat back to the bar, order another Seven and

Seven and wrap her arms around the first hot young dyke with blond hair. She imagined they'd dance for an hour, and then Eva would escort her out to her Porsche, an instant guarantee that they would go back to Eva's place.

She looked down and realized she was holding the oak box. The image of Eva with other women was one she tried to avoid. It was still too painful. Feeling like a closet drug addict, she pulled the vial from its box and stared at the swirling liquid. Her hands were shaking as she uncorked the vial and took a small sip. The pineapple flavor filled her mouth, and she felt the urge to sit down. She headed into an empty stall and planted herself on the toilet seat for a few seconds. It was like walking in a river against the current, her body engulfed by the surging rapids. She pulled out her cell phone, her resolve withering, but from somewhere a little voice was urging her to take action. She thought of Logan's smile and cascading hair as she reached into her purse for the slip of paper Logan had given her. There were three sevens in her phone number. *Could that be lucky?*

When Logan answered, she couldn't think of what to say.

"Hello?" Logan asked again. "Hello? Is that you, Grace?"

Hearing her name, realizing that Logan had not suddenly forgotten her or the proposition, bolstered her confidence. "Yes, Logan, it's me. Grace."

"I was wondering if you'd call. Have you changed your mind?"

"Well, I had a few questions—"

"Questions like what are the sleeping arrangements, when will I have you back to Phoenix and do I have a criminal record? Are those the kinds of questions you wanted to ask?"

"I think I'm good on the criminal record part," she said with a laugh. "I guess I just don't know what you're expecting of me."

"Nothing, really. I'd just like your company. Where are you?"

"I'm at the Monastery on Camelback."

"I'll be by in a little while."

She hung up before Grace could tell her that she needed to

go home and pack. When she returned to the table still holding her cell phone, Margo adopted a smug smile. "Somebody's going on a trip, right?"

Grace shook her head, unwilling to admit she'd swallowed the Root of Passion. "What am I going to do now?" she asked her friends. "She'll be here shortly, and I don't even have time to go home."

Margo waved a hand. "Honey, they have toiletries and clothes in Vegas. Live a little. Go spend some money at one of those boutiques on the strip. Find something sexy to wear to the wedding."

Suddenly panicked, she reached for her phone, but Margo grabbed her hand. "Don't. Have another glass of wine."

She obliged and relaxed. The room was warm, and she was suddenly feeling very comfortable with her decision to fly to Las Vegas with a beautiful woman. The conversation shifted to Margo's last trip to Paris and her strange liaison with her homophobic boss. It wasn't until Logan appeared at the table that she even remembered she was about to get on a plane.

"Hey," Logan said with a lazy smile. She glanced at Margo and Celeste and said, "We need to get to the airport."

Margo and Celeste quickly introduced themselves, and Grace excused herself again for the bathroom before they left. She lingered in the foyer a little, checking her hair and applying some lipstick. She was certainly not vain, but Logan's smile, combined with her attentive eyes—an obvious attribute of a photographer—made her more self-conscious than she'd ever been. She tugged at the sleeves of her maroon blouse and undid one more button. If Logan leaned over her shoulder during the flight, she would have a clear view down her shirt. *What are you doing, Grace?*

"Shut up," she said to the mirror and marched out to greet the weekend.

The anticipation she felt about their trip quickly dissipated as they drove to the airport in a taxi, Logan endlessly answering her cell phone—scheduling future shoots, talking to her two brothers about Chester and confirming with Kazmar's wedding coordinator about tomorrow's arrival at the McWhirter estate. By the time she finally disconnected her Bluetooth, they were being dropped at the curb, and then they began the harried calisthenics of airport arrival—check-in, security clearance and locating their gate.

Logan glanced at her watch. "We've still got forty minutes before we board. How about a cocktail? I'm dying to hear about the list."

She whirled to face her, clearly surprised. "How do you know about that?"

Logan laughed and pointed to a nearby lounge. Grace waited nervously in the booth while Logan visited the bar and returned with a beer and a merlot. She settled next to Grace and stroked her thigh, her eyes full of lust. Grace gripped the table and swallowed hard, feeling the river's current pull her toward Logan. She wanted to kiss her desperately, but now was not the time. *My God. We could wind up in the mile high club.*

She took a serious drink and faced her. "How do you know about the list?"

"Margo told me while you were in the bathroom. May I please see it?"

She balked initially, but when Logan snapped her fingers, she pulled out the piece of memo paper which was worn from repeated handling.

Logan reached for her reading glasses and surveyed the five items listed. "Let's see. Face a fear. What are you afraid of?"

She'd never really thought about it. "I don't know. The usual stuff, I guess. Death. Public speaking. Do those count?"

"I don't think that's what Margo's talking about." She grinned. "That's okay. I have a few ideas on that one. Next, have sex with a stranger." Her eyes bore into Grace's, and Grace resisted the urge to crawl into her lap. "We know that's already on the table," Logan said, in a silky voice. "The next two items actually could go together. Make a public spectacle of yourself and wear something sexy. Depending on what you choose, we could save some time there." She folded the paper back into fourths and returned it to her. "The only one I can't help you with is number five. I don't do relationships."

She raised an eyebrow. "You've never been in a relationship?"

Logan shook her head and sipped her beer. "I've been in enough relationships to know I don't do well in them. My career doesn't afford me much time with someone. I have a loft in New York, but I'm rarely there. I've learned commitment requires work, and it becomes a choice between traveling the world and staying in one place with one person." She shrugged. "I choose my career."

Grace was impressed by her honesty. "At least you know yourself and what you need."

"And what do *you* need, Grace? Do you like being alone?"

"I hate it," she said, entirely surprised when the words escaped her lips. *It's the potion. It's peeling away the cerebral cortex of my brain. I'm just saying whatever comes into my head.* She quickly held up a hand. "I should probably amend that somewhat. It's not like I'm desperate. I wouldn't settle for a woman who didn't share my values or my interests."

A slow smile crept over Logan's face. "It sounds like you know what you need, too, Dr. Owens. And I imagine there's already someone in your sights."

She shrugged. "Not really. My old girlfriend and I have a rather odd relationship, and my neighbors keep trying to set me up with a woman down the street who seems to be my exact opposite."

"And what is your exact opposite, Dr. Owens?"

She exhaled and thought of words to characterize Dina. "Let's see. Someone who's spontaneous, free-spirited, only has a GED, much younger and financially challenged."

"What's wrong with someone who never went to college?" Logan asked sharply.

She suddenly remembered Logan had no advanced degree. "I'm sorry. I didn't mean it like that." Logan said nothing but continued to stare. She felt she had to explain. "Look, it's just that my interests were all things I cultivated in college—my interests in art, philosophy and great literature. Most people who *went* to college don't like discussing those topics."

"Uh-huh. I see."

The conversation fizzled, and Grace felt horribly embarrassed. *She must think I'm a snob.* She watched the people hurry down the concourse. They clutched their boarding passes, their eyes upward, counting the gate signs. *They're different from me. They know where they're going and what awaits them at the destination.*

Logan interrupted her thoughts with a question she'd answered many times. "Why did you become a vascular surgeon?"

"I liked the intricacy and the precision. One of my professors in med school suggested it for me. He said I had the right temperament."

Logan chuckled and finished her drink. "I'll bet."

Before she could respond, the loudspeaker announced they were about to begin boarding the flight to Las Vegas.

They stepped into the long line, and she noticed those around her seemed to fit a certain stereotype: most were couples who she imagined were going to Vegas for a quick weekend of slots, sex and drinking. She was surprised that the hunky bodybuilder in front of them was alone. She guessed his perfectly toned physique got a little help from steroids, and several of the nearby straight women stole glances at him when they thought their husbands or boyfriends weren't looking. That ended when a six-foot bleach-blonde sidled up to him and possessively placed her hand in his back pocket. He wrapped a beefy arm around her bare midriff, for she wore a tiny tank top—braless, and the shortest miniskirt Grace had ever seen.

Logan and Grace exchanged glances. Several passengers were staring at the overtly sexual couple, who were now French kissing.

Logan whispered, "I think you're seeing an example of sexual dress and making a public spectacle of yourself, which, as I recall, are numbers three and four on your list."

"No," Grace said simply. "Not gonna happen."

Logan smiled pleasantly as the line began to move forward. "So," she said, brushing her hand against Grace's, "does this list need to be accomplished in order or can I improvise?"

Chapter Nine

Margo did a little dance as she headed into Destiny's, her feet automatically responding to the joyous rhythm of Pink's latest hit. Cushy, the bartender, caught her eye and waved.

"Margo!"

She leaned over the bar so Cushy could plant a kiss on each cheek. "Hey, sweetheart."

"I've missed you. How come you haven't been by?"

Cushy's dramatic frown was only half kidding, and she knew it. Cushy, whose nickname derived from her forty-two F bosom, was the owner of Destiny's, and she valued customer loyalty. She'd once berated a regular who'd started splitting her time between Destiny's and a competitor.

"I've been working, sweetie."

Cushy smiled and handed her a Cosmopolitan. "Enjoy."

She held the drink up in salute and sauntered toward a table of noisily gregarious women. She couldn't remember their names, but she'd seen two of them before. They folded her into their group and resumed their conversation about plastic surgery. Since three of them were model-thin, she wasn't surprised to hear that they favored a woman's right to augment. She only interjected her opinion twice, content with listening to their absolutely fascinating perspectives on the world. They were the drunk version of *The View*.

A Christina Aguilera song began, and the women flew from the table to the dance floor, leaving her with her thoughts. The plane would arrive soon in Vegas, and she imagined the trip could have upset Grace so much that she was purchasing her return ticket. On the other hand, Logan could have seduced her in the cab, and they were nestled between the hotel sheets. *That would be fabulous*. She guessed that Grace had swallowed the Root of Passion in the bathroom and called Logan. She had no idea if the potion really worked, but it was apparent that Grace thought it did. She bit her lip. That could be good or bad. Grace would take chances, but how far would she go?

Strong arms embraced her from behind, and she didn't need to turn around to know it was Joseph. His cologne announced his presence sight unseen.

"How are you, darling?" he asked, joining her.

She paused and thought about the question. "I don't know," she finally said. "There's some really weird shit going on in my life right now."

Joseph, who was used to dyke drama, sipped his martini, expressionless. "Go on. Dr. Joseph is listening."

"You're not a doctor," she said. "You're a chemist."

"Yes, but I'd play one on TV *so* well," he teased. "And I look ten times better than most of those doctors in that hospital. *Grey's Anatomy* totally over-beautified the medical profession."

"Can we get back to me?"

He nodded and returned to his drink. She told him about her visit to Rio, Chayna, the Root of Passion, Grace's rendezvous with Michelle and her own escapade in Paris with Norma. When she finished, he burst into laughter.

"Girl, what are you on?" he said. "That's the biggest fairy tale I've ever heard." He slapped the table and looked around. "Am I being punk'd?"

"It's true. This potion seems to have some bizarre effects."

He shook his head. "Margo, there's a simple explanation. In both circumstances, alcohol was involved, and it's been known to free people of their inhibitions, and liver function too. Your dictator boss was probably just responding to her own repressed lesbianism, and as for Grace and Michelle, that's a volcano that's been waiting to erupt for years!"

What he said was scientifically sound, but he hadn't seen the look in Norma's eyes when she begged for more sex after six times. To convince him, Margo would need more proof. A thought dawned on her.

"Okay, I understand your reasoning about the alcohol, but what if I told you that at this moment our friend Grace is flying to Las Vegas *with a gorgeous perfect stranger* to attend Kazmar Edens' wedding and do God knows what else."

His drink nearly slipped to the floor, but he caught it before too much of the precious liquor spilled over the rim. "Shit." He looked at her, unbelieving. "You're full of shit."

She pulled out her cell phone. "Shall we call her? By now her plane has probably landed."

"Who is this person? And how did Grace get an invite to the biggest celebrity wedding of the year? She's *Grace*. Grace doesn't go to flashy events. We couldn't even get her to go to that club opening last month."

"She went with Logan Brown, the photographer. Her father is one of Grace's patients. Apparently, they really hit it off. She wasn't going to go, but then she met me for a drink—"

"Again, more alcohol," he said.

"We only had one. Then she went to the bathroom and announced she was going. Explain that to me, mister scientist."

He shrugged. "I can't, but I don't think that automatically

means she's taking a magic potion."

He waved his hands around dramatically and she glowered. He wasn't going to believe her—unless he tried it himself. She pulled the oak box from her purse, and he watched as she withdrew the vial and took a small sip.

"There. I've proven that this isn't some type of horrible poison. How about you drink it?"

His eyes widened. "Me? You want me to drink that stuff?"

"Why not? You don't believe it has any effects, so what's the harm? Be a man and prove me wrong."

He eyed her shrewdly. "Let's go all the way to Fantasyland and take a ride on Dumbo. What if it does work—and I'm not saying it does. What the hell am I gonna do in a *lesbian* bar?"

She pointed at the dance floor. "See that group of women? They're definitely straight and just here to hide from the vultures."

He studied each of them, realizing that his eyes were glued to a curvaceous redhead who wore a purple silk dress with a plunging neckline.

Joseph believed he was ninety-percent straight, but he'd admitted to her that he periodically found himself attracted to a man. He felt a strong urge to care for a woman, get her pregnant and build a family. For some strange reason, he didn't have that urge with another man. Yet, when it came to dating, he was terribly shy. He talked a great game but when it came time to ask a woman out, he ran for the restroom.

He was still watching the redhead when the music changed to a slower beat. The five women danced with each other, laughing and carelessly stepping on each other's heels.

"You could go out there and sweep her off her feet."

"Yeah, right," he snorted.

"Joseph, watch."

She held up the vial, and his eyes followed the red and blue as it separated and remixed. He blinked several times, and she grinned.

"Pretty freaky, huh?"

He said nothing and just watched as she poured a small amount into his empty martini glass.

"Try it."

He glanced at the redhead, who was now dancing by herself, hugging her body as she swayed to the beat, and then he threw back the drink and licked his lips.

After several seconds, he shrugged. "I don't feel anything."

"Give it a little time."

The music shifted and a deep bass beat filled the room. He drummed his hand on the table, keeping time. Soon he was singing along with Katy Perry, and she grinned.

"Go get her, tiger," she said, pointing to the redhead.

He danced across the floor and joined the women, who immediately welcomed him. *Who wouldn't want to dance with a totally hot guy?* At first, he gave all of them his attention, but by the fourth song, he'd wrapped his arms around the redhead's waist and she was pressed against him. The other women returned to the table, twittering about their friend, Ainsley, and the handsome black stud sweeping her off her feet.

"Hey, that's my friend Joseph," Margo offered. "He's a great guy. Is she okay for him?"

"Oh, God, yes," a brunette with heavy red lipstick said. "Ainsley is like this super smart lawyer. She's the nicest person."

"And her family's incredibly rich," another said, and Margo noticed the huge rock on her ring finger.

"Why doesn't she have a boyfriend, or does she?"

The brunette said, "She spends most of her time at work. She only agreed to come with us tonight because we made her feel guilty about canceling on us again."

"Thanks," Margo said, moving away from the table and heading for the bar. Joseph led Ainsley off the dance floor and into a quiet booth that was just being vacated. It was clear she was just as interested in him as he was in her, and when he kissed her on the cheek—something shy Joseph would never do—she was convinced the Root of Passion was working.

She felt a sloppy tap on her shoulder and turned to face Eva.

Her entire face drooped and her expression was dark.

"Where's Grace?"

"I don't know."

"Yeah, you do. Did she go to Vegas for the weekend?"

She couldn't hide her surprise. "How did you know about that?"

"My telepathic powers," Eva slurred. "Is she with anyone?"

"Yeah, she's the guest of a world famous photographer."

Eva scowled. "Not Logan? Not the patient's daughter? Tell me it's not her."

She nodded. "She invited her to Kazmar Edens' wedding. Logan's taking the photographs."

"I thought you were her friend. You shouldn't have let her go."

Margo's anxiety peaked. "What do you know about Logan?"

At first Eva didn't respond, and Margo could tell she was entirely trashed. She opened her mouth to speak and seemed stuck. Finally she blurted, "She's bad news. I saw her at the hospital. I should have reported it…"

"Reported what?"

"She made a drug buy in the parking lot."

"Are you sure it was her?"

Eva nodded. "I was going to my car in the garage. I was on the ground floor and I looked over at the visitor's lot and I saw this other nurse, Paula, walking between the rows."

"How do you know it was Paula?"

"Paula's hard to miss. She's got this electric blue hair. They tried to get her to dye it but she threatened to sue, so they backed down. I saw her with Logan."

"Wait, wait. Go back. So, she's in the parking lot. Where was Logan?"

"She came up to her. I knew who she was. I'd seen Grace talking to her the day before, and I was a little jealous. So I stopped to watch them. I mean, maybe they were lovers and I didn't need to worry about her coming on to Grace. They stood there talking for a few seconds, making it look like Logan was lost. Paula kept pointing at the hospital as if she was giving directions, but she had something in her hand. And Logan got really close to her, and I saw a flash of green go into Paula's hand, and then they were both stuffing something into their pockets."

"How do you know it was drugs?"

"I guess I don't know for sure, but there've been rumors flying about Paula for months. It's just nobody can prove it."

She felt her chest tighten. *Don't panic. She's drunk and jealous. She couldn't have been very close to see what was really happening. And even if Logan was buying drugs, that doesn't mean she's an awful person and would hurt Grace.*

Eva closed her eyes and started to fall backwards but Margo caught her in time. "Eva, wake up," she said harshly. She shook her until her eyes opened again. "I'm taking you home."

Margo had been to Eva's place many times with Grace. The women had never lived together, a blessing in her opinion. When they broke up it was quick and painless, particularly since Grace didn't seem to realize it had occurred for nearly two weeks.

Eva's condo was a few miles from the hospital in an old part of central Phoenix. The single-story units sat in a rectangle, framing a beautiful courtyard full of lush shrubbery, plants and waterfalls. Weeping willows and bottle brush trees drooped over the roofs, perpetually shading the entire structure. It always reminded her of perfect solitude and she understood why Eva refused to leave, even for a girlfriend.

The condo was spacious, a throwback to a time when square footage wasn't a luxury. She half-carried, half-walked Eva to her bedroom and tossed her onto the giant futon. *Grace hated this thing.* She'd listened to her endless whining every time it was her turn to stay at Eva's. She'd rant about back support and comfort, but she never told Eva how much she detested the sleeping arrangements.

Eva turned over and groaned. "How did I get here?"

"I brought you home. Why are you drunk?" she thought to ask.

She gave a slight shrug. "I can't explain it. I saw Grace and she told me she might be going to this wedding and the next thing I know, my car is sitting in front of Destiny's. I didn't plan it."

"Hmm. I see," Margo said, understanding the situation entirely.

She glanced over at Eva's nightstand and her suspicions were confirmed. Perched on the edge, in the place of prominence reserved for favorite photos, sat a five by seven of Eva and Grace, staring into each other's eyes, moments before their lips met in a kiss.

Chapter Ten

As the plane descended, Grace was amazed by the millions of lights clustered in the vast desert. *I wonder if they can see this place in space.* She'd never been to Las Vegas. She hated to gamble, drank minimally and had little interest in all-you-can-eat buffets. She'd heard the strip was scummy, filled with sights and smells that tourists wouldn't tolerate in any other city. Yet, excitement twirled inside her as she recognized the Eiffel Tower and the Paris hotel, where, according to Logan, they would be staying. She peered through the tiny window, Logan's chin resting against her shoulder.

"All that debauchery," Logan said. "Just waiting for us."

They debarked and Logan navigated the airport terminal like an expert, although she said she'd only been to McCarran International Airport one other time.

"The secret is following the signs. So many people don't read," she muttered as she claimed her luggage from the carousel.

Grace felt dreadfully out of place since she didn't even have a toothbrush. Logan must have sensed her anxiety after she'd loaded her five bags onto a cart. She threw an arm around Grace and said, "Don't worry. I'll take care of you."

She gazed out the cab's window as they slowly meandered down the busy strip. She couldn't believe the thousands of people crowding the narrow sidewalks. Most were obviously tourists, who insisted on stopping anywhere to take a picture of the Luxor's pyramid, the fountains at the Bellagio or the classic Roman architecture of Caesar's Palace. As their cab turned into the Paris, she craned her neck to see the Eiffel Tower.

"There's a French restaurant up there," Logan whispered. "Do you like French food?"

Logan's warm breath caressed her face and she closed her eyes a moment, enjoying her nearness. She was starting to lose control, certain that the Root of Passion was churning through her body, responding to the millions of lights and sounds around her. She turned to Logan and licked her lips.

"I love French food," she replied.

Logan smiled and glanced down at her cleavage.

I'm glad to see you noticed.

Again she pictured herself standing in a river, the current overtaking her, peeling away the inhibitions that shackled her. She reached for Logan, tucking a stray wisp of her hair behind her ear.

Her sigh was audible. "I see where this is going. Okay," she said.

When the cab dropped them at the front of the hotel, a bellman appeared immediately to take Logan's luggage. Free of the bags—except her prized camera case that she wouldn't turn over to anyone—Logan took her hand and led her through the lobby, which she quickly realized was unlike any place she'd ever been.

"They've recreated Paris," she said, noticing that they were indeed surrounded by a miniature version of the City of Lights, including a bright blue sky overhead. Logan led her past replicas of the Louvre and the Arc de Triomphe. "This is unbelievable," she decided.

"Are you hungry? Logan asked. "We could try the restaurant," she added, pointing to the base of the Eiffel Tower and the elevator that would take them to the eleventh floor.

She shook her head. "I'm starving, but I can't go to a fancy place looking like this." She glanced down at her linen slacks and the simple blouse she'd changed into after work.

Logan laughed. "This is Vegas, Grace. No one would care. Look at me."

Logan wore cargo pants and a collared shirt, minus her usual vest.

"I wouldn't feel comfortable," she said, and Logan smiled.

"Then we need to get you some clothes."

She took her hand and led her to Rue de la Paix, an avenue of shops. They found a boutique with a difficult French name, and Logan wasted no time finding a saleslady who gave Grace a long look before she began pulling dresses from the rack, never bothering to ask her size. She was shuttled into a dressing room by another saleswoman speaking French, and dresses began appearing over the door. She took one look at a price tag and almost fainted.

As if she could read her mind, Logan's voice called from the other side, "Don't worry about the cost, Grace. This is my treat. Well, it's probably Kazmar's treat actually, since he told me I could bring a friend. Make sure you find something for tonight and a dress for the wedding. A few casual items would be good, too. I'll be back in a while."

"Don't you want to see what I pick?" Grace asked.

"No, I hate shopping. Surprise me."

Never in her life had Grace tried on so many beautiful clothes so quickly. The dresses seemed to be of two types: incredibly sexy and unbelievably elegant. She imagined Logan had coached the salesladies, who helped her settle on a shimmering green cocktail dress for their trip to the restaurant and a more conservative navy blue dress with a classic A-line style that accentuated her curves. Matching shoes, bras, panties, hose and bags appeared immediately, and while she dressed for dinner, the ladies thrust several pairs of pants and blouses under her nose for her approval. By the time an hour had passed, she had nearly doubled her wardrobe and owned enough cosmetics to start her own line. She couldn't imagine how Logan would ever justify the bill to Kazmar.

When she appeared outside the shop wearing the green dress, several passersby gawked, and one man smiled flirtatiously. She heard a click and saw a flash before she noticed Logan a few yards away, lowering her camera. She'd changed into blue slacks and a tailored white shirt.

"You look absolutely beautiful," she said, kissing her hand.

"I thought you hated shopping."

"I do. But I couldn't imagine being seen with you looking like a bum."

Logan wrapped a possessive arm around her waist and escorted her toward the elevator. People continued to stare, and she wasn't certain if her dress or Logan's overt behavior was the cause. She chose to believe it was the former and not the latter, because during the cab ride she'd seen several gay couples holding hands and kissing along the strip. And her dress was certainly eye-catching, with a plunging front and back. There was no way she could wear her bra, which she'd left for the salesladies to send to her room with the other purchases.

As they ascended, Logan's fingertips traced a circle against the naked flesh of her back, and she nearly gasped. She couldn't look at her, for she knew the radiant green eyes would pull her into the river, and they'd be French kissing in the French elevator.

In the restaurant the Root of Passion heightened her sensory awareness and her appreciation of the food and her surroundings. The view of the Bellagio fountains was magnificent, the food tasted exquisite, and whenever Logan innocently touched her arm her entire body reacted. Maybe it was the expensive French wine Logan ordered, for she was tipsy after two glasses. She worried she was giggling like a schoolgirl and making a spectacle of herself, but Logan only smiled at her, studied her, and much to her great pleasure, surveyed her like a photographic subject.

They shared an amazing pastry called a dariole for dessert, and Grace found herself swallowing hard, wondering what the rest of the evening would bring.

After dinner, Logan insisted that they stroll through the resort, arm in arm. She seemed entirely at ease, regaling Grace with stories of her travels, and Grace's anxiety lessened as her attraction to Logan increased. *She must have a girlfriend in every city. She is utterly charming.*

It was nearly twelve thirty when they boarded the elevator, headed for the eighth floor. Alone, Logan pulled Grace against her, whispering kisses against her neck. Grace stiffened immediately and Logan lifted her head.

"A little too fast," she said, stepping away. "You're just so amazing and incredibly beautiful, too."

Grace laughed. "You are such a flatterer."

Logan shook her head. "No, I just have exquisite taste in women." She kissed her hand, and Grace thought she would faint.

When the doors opened, Grace quickly stepped out and hurried down the hallway in search of eight twenty-one. She waited patiently for Logan to join her, but Logan sauntered down the hallway slowly, as if to preserve the evening and the moments they'd shared. She took a deep breath as Logan slid the key card into the lock.

She wasn't disappointed. Kazmar had secured a lovely suite, one with a sitting room and two bedrooms. Not only would Grace have her own bed, she would have privacy. They toured the suite, and she noticed all of her packages had been placed on the sofa in her bedroom. A single bag sat on Logan's bed next to her pile of luggage.

"What else did you buy?"

"Why don't you open it?" Logan replied in a husky voice.

"It's for you."

Grace pulled a thin rectangular box from the bag and discovered a lacy teddy inside. Her mouth went dry as she deduced the ramifications. Logan hoped she would wear this for her, and she suddenly realized she had not purchased any sleepwear.

Logan's arms wrapped around her from behind, and her lips rested against Grace's ear. "I wanted you to have a choice. Wear this or sleep in the nude. Frankly, I'm good with either."

Her heart was pounding and she turned to face her. The river was gone. *Why wasn't the Root of Passion working?* "I can't. I just can't."

She ran from the room and into her own, practically slamming the door in the process. She dropped the box on the bed and the sexy lingerie seemed to jump out onto the bedspread. It was dusty rose, a complement to her skin color. She turned away and busied herself by hanging up all of the fine clothes she'd acquired. She wondered what Logan was doing. She didn't hear the TV or Logan talking on her cell. Maybe she should book a flight home.

She paced the room, wringing her hands until a knock sounded. Logan opened the door and stood in the doorway, arms folded. She'd changed into her sleep attire—a tank top and men's underwear. She looked sexy and Grace felt warm all over.

"I just wanted to say good-night. I'm sorry I pushed you so hard, and I hope you're not angry."

She sighed in relief. "I'm not. I was worried you were angry with me."

Logan simply shook her head. "No." She closed the door, saying, "Good-night," before it shut.

Grace glanced about the beautiful room, the silence growing around her. She hung up the green dress and decided to shower, grateful to see an entire set of toiletries on the immense bathroom counter. She felt refreshed, covered in the hotel's plush bath towels. She pampered herself with some exquisite body lotion and dried her hair. Letting the towels drop to the floor, she inspected the teddy again. The fine silk caressed her fingertips, and she longed to have it against her body.

It fit beautifully and when she looked in the mirror she felt incredibly sexy. She turned and judged her body from different angles, pleased with what the teddy revealed—and hid. Should she show Logan? After all, she was the one who purchased it. *C'mon, Grace, if you leave this room you'll be flat on your back in a matter of minutes—on the sofa, the floor or Logan's bed.*

She automatically pulled the list from her purse and reread it. The words seemed to dare her to take a risk. She imagined if she returned from Vegas without accomplishing a single objective, Margo and Michelle would spend the rest of the year, if not her life, chastising her for the lost opportunity. Without wasting another moment, she withdrew the vial from the oak box and took a serious drink, noticing half the potion was gone. She leaned against the mirror and closed her eyes, letting her senses overwhelm her. She pictured Logan in the doorway, her eyes smoldering.

Lust washed over her, and she quickly applied some scorching red lipstick and headed out into the living room. It was dark, but she could see a slash of light from underneath Logan's bedroom door. She didn't bother to knock, but instead grabbed the door handle and appeared. Logan's eyes shot up from the book she was reading in bed. Grace noticed the title, *Thus Spoke Zarathustra* by Nietzsche, and she suddenly felt terrible about her college comments. If she was reading Nietzsche she could certainly hold her own in a philosophical conversation.

Logan rose and went to her, shedding her clothing as she approached. She pulled Grace against her and wrapped her in a tight embrace, her hands caressing Grace's buttocks.

"I thought this was the smoothest silk I'd ever felt," she whispered in her ear. "I want to feel it against my skin, too."

Logan claimed her mouth in kisses. They were luscious and divine, and she tasted wonderful. Grace was so intent on savoring her sweet lips that she didn't notice her tiny panties had dropped to the floor until Logan's fingers swept across her center. She moaned slightly and Logan immediately took advantage.

"I want you," Logan said.

In seconds Grace was prostrate on the bed, staring at the gorgeous crown molding that lined the ceiling. Logan was kissing and caressing her entire body while she melted into the expensive sheets. She pulled off her top as Logan's lips approached her waiting nipples.

"God, that feels incredible," she murmured, closing her eyes.

"What do you want me to do?" Logan asked.

"Anything you want."

Logan complied, and the river appeared again, swirling around her, drowning her in ecstasy.

Chapter Eleven

When Grace awoke, she felt disoriented until she remembered she was in Logan's bed. She blinked and Logan hovered above, wearing a hotel bathrobe and holding the list.

"I guess you can cross off number two," she said rather smugly. "Now we just need to have you face a fear, make a public spectacle of yourself and wear something sexy." She glanced at the discarded teddy and shook her head. "And before you say anything, I don't think that's what your friend meant. She wants you hot, and she wants you to turn heads in public."

"Great," Grace said, unwilling to debate the list when she wasn't fully awake.

Logan sat on the edge of the bed and held her hand. "How did you sleep?"

"Soundly. At least after you stopped making me come."

"Ah, yes." Logan bent down and kissed her deeply. "I wish

I could claim to be an extraordinary lover, but it wasn't that difficult. All I had to do was touch you and you were practically ready to orgasm."

The Root of Passion. She didn't say anything about the potion, certain that at least a part of her was aroused by Logan's incredible body and ability in bed.

"I hope you enjoyed it, too," she said, unsure if the potion improved her prowess as a lover.

Logan laughed and stroked her neck tenderly. "It was wonderful. You give as good as you get. Now, it's almost ten, and I need to be at the estate in two hours. We need to get moving."

But heat was already coursing through Grace, and her body responded to Logan's lingering touch. She placed Logan's hand on her breast and covered it with her own.

"We have a little time, don't we? I promise I can be ready quick."

Logan discarded the robe and rolled on top of Grace.

"If I'm late, you get to explain this to Kazmar."

The wedding was scheduled for two, which gave Grace ample time to roam about the estate while Logan prepared her cameras and examined the makeshift photo studio that had been assembled for the wedding party pictures.

Grace had been inside two mansions, but nothing equaled the opulence of the McWhirter estate. Vases, sculptures, tapestries and paintings covered the walls and lined the cavernous corridors. Although McWhirter had made his millions in the dot com industry, his passion was obviously art, and he favored no particular medium. *It's like being in a museum.*

At one point she got lost, her attention focused on a wall of modern art rather than the path she was taking. Two hallways forked in different directions and she immediately chose the one on the right, thinking that she could doubleback toward the main part of the house. Instead, she found herself dead-ending at a door. The knob turned easily, and in a moment, she was standing in Linus McWhirter's massive garage.

Automobiles stood at attention in two rows, and she realized there were probably twenty cars total. *This place is bigger than my entire neighborhood.* She wandered down the center aisle between the cars, admiring the sleek and powerful Bentleys, Porsches, Mercedes, and others she couldn't name. Against a far wall sat a row of motorcycles and her untrained eye recognized that the bikes were a chronological history of Harley-Davidson. The first motorcycle was ancient while the last one was obviously a top of the line late-model edition. The entire collection was probably worth a fortune.

"Do you ride?"

She jumped, startled by the voice. A woman in a UNLV baseball cap and coveralls approached. She was pleasant looking and wisps of chestnut brown hair fell about her smiling face.

"I'm sorry if I scared you. I'm Penny."

She held out her hand, which was free of grease and dirt.

"Hi, I'm Grace. I'm sorry to intrude. I think I'm lost."

"That's okay. You're here for the wedding?"

"I am, but I'm not really a guest. I'm a friend of the photographer's."

"You mean that hot blonde in the tight black pants and polka dot vest?"

Grace blushed at the description of Logan, who had chosen to wear a tasteful vest covered in small dots. She'd told Grace she needed to stand out, so that people could find her immediately, in case a moment needed to be captured instantly for posterity.

"Yeah, that's Logan. I'm with her."

Penny eyed her shrewdly and then pointed at the motorcycle collection. "I saw you admiring the Harleys, but you still haven't answered my question. Do you ride?"

"Who me? No. I've only been on one once. Too dangerous."

A slow smile crept across Penny's face. "Really?"

"Oh, yes. I'm a doctor, and I can't tell you how many motorcycle accidents I've covered. They're always horrible, especially when the riders haven't worn helmets."

"It's worth the risk," Penny said. "I agree with you about the helmet part, but there's nothing like a great ride on the open road."

"I'll take your word for it. I should probably get back to the wedding. Can you tell me how to find my way back?"

Penny moved closer to Grace, hands deep in her pockets. She rocked back on her heels and looked at the ground. "You know, I could show you how to ride. I'm sure you'd like it once you tried it."

"I doubt it. Thanks for the offer, though."

"Are you sure? There's nothing like straddling a bike, the engines purring beneath you, the wind pressed against your body. It's the *second* best thing in the world."

Grace swallowed hard, rather certain she knew what the *first* best thing in the world was. She watched Penny's crooked smile, an open invitation, and the river opened up again in front of her. She pictured herself sitting behind Penny, her arms wrapped around her waist as they coasted down an open highway.

"I'm only here until tomorrow," she said, not believing the words were coming from her mouth.

"Tomorrow would be great. I'm free. I'd love to take you and your photographer friend out. Does she ride?"

"I'm not sure." But Grace imagined there wasn't much Logan hadn't experienced during her life.

"Well, you talk to her and call me. Do you have a cell?"

She retrieved her phone from her purse, her hand grazing the oak box and the Root of Passion. *Could the potion have anything to do with my sudden insanity?*

Penny punched her number into Grace's contact list and returned the phone, grinning. "I think—no, I *know* we'll have fun tomorrow."

"Are you sure Mr. McWhirter will let us borrow his motorcycles?"

"I think it'll be fine," Penny said. "He doesn't own the motorcycles. They belong to me."

"They do?"

"Yeah. I'm Penny McWhirter, Linus's daughter."

Chapter Twelve

By Saturday afternoon Margo wasn't sure if she should be worried or relieved. Eva's information about Logan was disturbing, and her opinion of Logan certainly had changed—and not for the better. Grace would have a fit if she knew Logan was a drug user. That was an absolute deal-breaker for her. Margo had flipped open her cell phone at least ten times, but she couldn't bring herself to call Grace. *What would I do? Warn her? Tell her to fly home immediately?*

"This is my fault," she mumbled as she pulled into Grace's driveway. "If I hadn't encouraged her and bought that potion…"

Grace had been gone for almost eighteen hours, and she hadn't left Margo any frantic messages about her terrible weekend or pleaded with her to come to the airport and pick her up. Margo didn't know what to make of it. She wasn't used to

Grace being away, especially under such unusual circumstances. *She* was the one who traveled while Grace stayed in Phoenix, keeping an eye on her condo, watering her plants and preventing the world from devolving into chaos for Margo. At least, that was how it had always been. She counted on Grace to keep her sane. It was Grace's unspoken job, and now she'd abandoned her.

That's rather selfish, she thought, particularly since she'd helped create the list. Still, she worried about Logan's influence. Was she having any fun? Was she having *too much* fun? Would she be ready to kill her when she returned? She was curious as hell to know what was going on but she worried that if they spoke she'd feel obligated to share Eva's story about Logan.

Grace's BMW was still in the driveway, driven back from the Monastery by one of the waiters, and so was her newspaper. She would never leave her paper in the driveway. Margo found the spare key under the frog sculpture and deposited the paper and the mail on Grace's spotless dining room table. She looked around the pristine house, both envious and repulsed. She would never have a house this clean or orderly, and a part of her was grateful.

"Only a sick mind is this neat," she mumbled.

She debated whether to snoop. Rarely did she get a chance to get this much dirt on a friend, but again, Grace had few secrets—of this she was sure. Grace was the straight arrow, free of skeletons in her closet.

Her phone chimed and Joseph's picture appeared on her display. "Hey, lover."

He laughed. "I wouldn't go that far, but Ainsley is a terrific woman. We sat in that booth and talked until Cushy threw us out."

"Talked? I give you a magic sex potion and all you did was talk? Or did you take her home and show her what she'd been missing?"

"You mean my handsome black ass?"

She chuckled. It was one of their ongoing jokes that white women always stared at Joseph more than black women did.

"Sorry to disappoint you, but we both kept our clothes on last night. I am a gentleman, you know."

"Absolutely. If you were an asshole, I couldn't see you socially. So is there anything to tell?"

"We're going out again tonight and I just wanted to thank you for helping me. I don't know if there's anything to that Root of Passion stuff, but I'm having a second date with an amazing woman."

"Well, you're welcome. Just call me the Sex Samaritan. I go about the world helping those with sexual needs and righting the unjust wrongs."

She heard a knock on Grace's back door and a young woman appeared and called, "Hello?"

She recognized Dina, Grace's neighbor. "I gotta go."

"Hi, I'm Dina. I live down the street. I saw your car and the open back door and I thought I should check."

A long-handled trowel protruded from the side pocket of Dina's overalls. She was prepared for action if necessary. Margo liked that. She stuck out her hand.

"I'm Margo. Grace's best friend. I was waiting in the car when your dog sacked Grace on the lawn the other night."

Dina automatically looked down and scratched the side of her head. "I felt really bad about that. Pepper's usually much better behaved."

"I don't mean to be blunt, Dina, but from where I was sitting, you seemed to enjoy the view."

Dina opened her mouth to speak but nothing came out. She took a deep breath and said, "Well, she's very beautiful, and when she had one of those, what would you call—wardrobe malfunctions—it was hard to miss."

"So you think she's attractive."

Her cheeks reddened, and Margo imagined she was making her quite uncomfortable. *So be it, if it helps Grace find the right woman.*

"Of course. I mean, it's not like I've ever told her. We hardly see each other except for a friendly wave." She looked around.

"Since we're having such a frank talk, where is she? Her routine seems pretty solid."

"She took a trip."

"Really?"

Margo laughed at her surprise. "I know it sounds unusual. Grace isn't one to travel on short notice."

"Yeah, she hasn't struck me as a spur-of-the-moment kind of person."

Margo realized that they'd slid into the chairs surrounding Grace's dining room table. She might as well continue the conversation. "Grace is definitely a creature of habit, but this time it was worth it. She was invited to Kazmar Edens' wedding."

Dina raised her eyebrows. "Seriously? She must know some pretty important people."

"Friend of a friend," Margo replied, deciding instantly that she liked Dina and wanted Grace to dump Logan. Eva would have to get in line—after Dina. *It would be good for Grace to have choices.*

She leaned back and crossed her arms. "So what's your story, Dina? It's my job as Grace's best friend to interview any potential dates."

"I work for a landscaper. We mainly do resorts."

Blue collar, she thought. *That's definitely a yin to Grace's yang.* "Do you like it?"

She shrugged. "It's a job. I don't love it, but I'm happy to go to work in the morning. A lot of people can't say that."

"How long have you worked in landscaping?"

"About a year. I assume you want to know what I did before that?"

"Of course."

"I worked at Starbuck's, and before that I was a baggage handler for Southwest, and before that I was a wrangler at a ranch in Colorado."

"Anything else?"

She laughed. "There were several other little jobs. I did whatever I could to pay my rent and avoid college."

Her radar perked up. *Maybe this wouldn't be such a great idea.* "What do you have against college?"

"Nothing, as long as I don't have to go. It's great for everyone else, but not for me."

"Did you ever try it?"

She looked away, frowning. "I went to NYU for a year."

Okay, she's back in the game. "Wow. That's a great school. What was your major?"

Staring out the window, she said, "I didn't declare one. My father wanted me to go into finance or law, so he didn't approve of the philosophy and women's studies courses I took. When I refused to follow his prescribed program of study, he cut me off."

Margo had heard similar stories before. "Shit. That sucks."

"Dropping out didn't suck. It was losing my parents' faith that really sucked."

"I'll bet."

Grace's absence filled the room, and Margo rose to go, uncomfortable with the silence and the intimate conversation. She wasn't good at sharing feelings. *That's what Grace does best.*

An idea came to her. "Hey, do you think you could keep an eye on the place for me and pick up her newspaper in the morning? She'll be home late tomorrow night but I have to work in a few hours and I know she wouldn't want it to sit in the driveway."

"Sure not a problem," she said with a wink.

This woman could be the one for Grace.

They both headed for the door, Margo locking up behind her. She showed Dina where the spare key was hidden and headed for her car. The conversation felt undone, as if there was more to say.

"And just so you know," she called, "Grace is someone who needs a woman who'll make the first move. She's not one to take the initiative. You know what I mean?"

Dina nodded. "Yeah, I do. I've known a lot of women who were shy."

She thought of the Root of Passion and the weekend in

Vegas. "That's a good word for Grace, but I think this trip will change her. The predictable Grace will be replaced by someone much more exciting."

Chapter Thirteen

The wedding proved to be the most lavish affair Grace had ever attended. No detail was left unplanned, and she imagined Kazmar's wedding coordinator drank heavily just to relieve the stress. The couple was to be married in McWhirter's great room, which had been fashioned after an English church complete with large stained-glass windows, dark oak beams, and an elevated platform that was decorated with flowers and would serve as an altar.

The reception would be outdoors in the lush garden. Disregarding the desert climate, endless rows of flowers and shrubs surrounded a perfect tiff lawn that probably needed constant watering. A sea of tables filled with canapés, lobster and champagne awaited the guests after they celebrated the marriage. Penguin-like waiters huddled with their captains, listening to the instructions that would ensure the service looked like a choreographed ballet. Her stomach rumbled but she imagined if she swiped a salmon roll from a tray she would be taken to the ground by the harried coordinator who continued to talk on his Bluetooth, bark orders at the dining captains and scribble messages to his assistant.

She returned to the hall and planted herself in the back, attempting to be unobtrusive while she gaped at the A-list celebrities who quickly filled up both sides of the aisle. Brad and Angelina, Will and Jada and George Clooney, along with his latest girlfriend, looked more glamorous in public than in photos.

Logan moved throughout the crowd effortlessly, like an unnoticed fly on the wall, snapping pictures of unsuspecting guests, changing lenses and ordering her assistant to reposition lights as directed. She was sleek and stealthy, the camera an extension of her arm, and obviously quite comfortable in her surroundings, even though she'd never been inside the hall. Grace imagined she was an expert at melding into her environment. At one point, she looked up and met her stare. A slight smile crossed her face and she winked.

A hush fell over the crowd as a clock struck two. The harpist, who had played mood music for the gathering guests, finished her song and the room went quiet. The string quartet began "Ode to Joy" and the wedding party entered. It wasn't until Lena Lago entered that all the heads turned. The Brazilian beauty wore a dress that Grace suspected equaled her own salary for a year. It was designed with thousands of beads and what appeared to be small diamonds. The low-cut bodice accentuated her bust, which Grace was certain had been augmented by a great plastic surgeon.

The ceremony was over quickly, and she marveled that it took longer to gather the guests inside and parade the wedding party down the aisle than it did to perform the wedding.

Everyone quickly filed out behind the elated bride and groom and headed for the lobster and champagne. She stayed behind as

Logan finished capturing shots of the departing guests.

"Well, what did you think?" she asked Grace.

"Makes me glad I'm a lesbian."

Logan chuckled and shifted her camera bag to her shoulder. "So you'd never want a wedding like this?"

"No. I'm not interested in lavish parties. Even if I could get married, I'd rather fly up here and let Elvis marry us. No fuss, no hassle."

Logan slung her arm around Grace's shoulder and pecked her on the cheek. "I like the way you think, Dr. Owens. If I were the marrying type, which I'm not, I'd opt for the same thing."

Grace fell into her eyes again, just as she had when they'd made love. Logan made no move to remove her arm or take off for the reception. Instead, she pulled her into a passionate kiss, one that made Grace's knees buckle.

"Aren't you supposed to be photographing the reception now?"

"Yes," Logan said, sighing. "But all work and no play…well, you know how the rest of it goes." She touched Grace's cheek with the back of her hand. "I don't think I told you how special last night was to me."

"I'll bet you say that to all the girls."

She shook her head. "No, I've never said that to anyone. I avoid those types of statements because women tend to get their hopes up. They think they can change me, and I'll leave my job for them."

"Have you ever come close?"

A sad smile crossed her face. "Only once. A long time ago." She took a deep breath and glanced toward the open door. "Well, I better get back to work. C'mon, I'll introduce you to some people. You'll love Kazmar. He's a great guy."

She extended her arm, and Grace took it. As they entered the reception, heads turned toward them, and Grace was certain many of the guests thought they were a couple. *Could it possibly happen?*

Chapter Fourteen

Kazmar reached the end of another story—for he'd told at least a dozen—and the entire table, including Grace, burst into laughter. Somehow he and Lena had planted themselves in the back where Logan had situated her while she worked. She had introduced her to Kazmar and Lena, who were unpretentious and gracious, and they had asked her to join them at a table that was filled with Kazmar's childhood buddies, people who knew him when he was Kevin Martin, before he became Kazmar, the Sexiest Man Alive, according to *People* magazine.

She was grateful for the company, although she wished the guy next to her, Eric, would quit putting his arm around her. Other than that little annoyance she was having a delightful time. Once in a while she would look up and see Logan working the room, talking to the guests. Some women openly flirted with her, which really didn't surprise Grace at all. She was beautiful and any straight woman with the slightest bent would give her time.

"Grace, I hope Kaz isn't boring you?" Lena asked.

She looked over her shoulder, realizing that Lena was standing behind her. She immediately stood, thankful to be rid of Eric.

"Not hardly. I'm having a wonderful time, and I'm glad to be here."

Pleased, Lena took her arm and walked her to a corner. "I think you're gorgeous, and I can tell Logan is smitten with you."

Her cheeks reddened. "I don't know about that. Logan is certainly a free spirit. I think she likes a lot of women."

"She certainly does," Lena said knowingly.

"I didn't realize you two were friends."

"Oh, yes. She photographed my very first shoot in Brazil six years ago. We got along famously. Perhaps too famously," she quickly added. When Grace said nothing, Lena whispered, "We were lovers for a while."

"Oh." She hoped she didn't sound too surprised. Why should she be? Both women were very attractive, and, as a model, Lena had to be indebted to the photographer who launched her career.

"When Kaz and I decided to get married, she was the only photographer I wanted. She understands me."

"She's incredibly talented," Grace agreed.

Both of them glanced at Logan who was talking to a thin brunette with shoulder-length straight hair. Grace immediately recognized Penny McWhirter's high cheekbones. Logan and Penny were laughing, and they looked toward her at the same time and smiled. *Is she another lover, too?*

Lena touched her arm and said, "You might want to go over and join them. There's nothing like a ménage a trois to spice up your life."

She turned to Kazmar, and Grace joined Penny and Logan. Penny flashed a friendly smile and Grace realized how striking she was without the ball cap covering her face. She wore a shimmering red cocktail dress which was so short that Grace could see most of her upper thigh. *She certainly has incredible legs.*

"You look a little different without your coveralls," Grace said.

"I thought I'd change before I rubbed elbows with the rich and famous."

"Have you two met?" a confused Logan asked.

"She wandered into the garage today," Penny explained. "I have a collection of motorcycles and I told her we'd go riding tomorrow if you're up for it."

"I'd love to." She looked at Grace. "I think we can convince Grace with a little arm twisting." She felt Logan's arm wrap possessively around her waist, a gesture that Penny watched carefully.

"Are you almost done?" Grace asked.

"Yeah," Logan said. She looked around the room. Three hours had passed since Kazmar and Lena had wed and most of the guests had left, particularly the A-listers who only stayed long enough to be seen and to be considered polite. "I think I can pack it in."

"Then how about coming to the after-party? Kazmar and Lena have invited their select friends inside for a special toast and some really good eats."

"And this wasn't?" Grace asked. "This is the nicest reception I've ever attended."

Penny and Logan exchanged knowing glances. "Grace, there's nice and then there's obscene," Logan explained. "What you've witnessed was expected, and the food and drink were palatable, but the rich know how to keep the good stuff to themselves."

Grace allowed Penny and Logan to lead her inside—back to the great room where, just a few hours before, Kazmar and Lena had promised to love each other for eternity. She had been impressed that the room looked so much like a country church in England. Yet, as they stepped through the heavy oak doors, she realized that in a short time the room had been transformed into a gambling hall, complete with craps tables, roulette wheel and blackjack dealers. A metal band, whose song she recognized even though she couldn't name it, cavorted across the converted altar, their electric guitars reverberating throughout the room. *I'm surprised they don't crack the stained glass.*

The penguin-like waiters and waitresses had also changed—their crisp uniforms discarded for much, much more casual attire—golden thongs. They wore nothing else, and she could tell the beautifully busted women had added a second layer of makeup and hot pink lipstick. A crowd was assembling near the doorway, and when Kazmar and Lena entered, everyone applauded. Gone were his tuxedo and her expensive dress. He wore jeans and a muscle shirt while she sported a low-cut spaghetti strap tank top that left little to the imagination and very short shorts that revealed the curves of her tanned buttocks. The band struck up a hit song, and Lena grabbed her new husband and dragged him out to dance. She thrust her hips and breasts at him, until he finally pulled her into a long kiss and the crowd roared again.

A chesty redheaded waitress bounced in front of them with Dom Perignon. "Champagne?"

All three of them took a flute and Penny raised her glass. "To Kazmar, Lena and a great party. I love the rich and am proud to be one of them."

They sipped their champagne and Grace immediately recognized the difference between the reception champagne and what she enjoyed now. It was the most eloquent drink she'd ever savored, and it was going straight to her head.

"Have you ever played roulette, Grace?" Penny asked.

"No."

Penny grabbed her hand and pulled her toward the table. Grace glanced over her shoulder and caught Logan's slight good-bye wave. Before she knew what was happening, she was making bets on red and black with chips that seemed to magically appear in front of her. Penny remained close, whispering advice and explanations. Often, her hand would graze Grace's back, and she thought of the Root of Passion deep in her purse. *What were Penny's expectations? Where did Logan disappear to?*

She looked down and realized she'd been steadily winning and had amassed a large pile of fifty-dollar chips. "Is this real money?"

Penny offered a lopsided grin. "Of course it's real, but it's not your money. It's mine. Don't worry about it."

She automatically stepped away. "Oh, no. Then you should be placing the bets."

Penny placed her hands on Grace's arms and stroked them gently. "Are you kidding? You're my good luck charm. This is the best case of beginner's luck that I've ever seen!" She leaned toward her, and she knew she was about to be kissed.

"Hey, you two! Play the game or get a room!" one of the other players shouted, and Penny quickly pulled away, her cheeks red.

She motioned they'd cash in, obviously embarrassed, and an assistant at the table swiftly stacked the chips into equal piles, counted them, and handed over a wad of bills. After they stepped away from the table, she said, "Logan mentioned you like art. Do you like Jackson Pollock?"

She nodded. "He's my favorite."

"Then let me show you something."

She took her hand and led her through a back door and down a hallway to a spiral staircase. Grace followed her up to the second floor and down another hallway to a set of double doors.

"It's in my room," Penny said, opening the doors with a flourish.

Her jaw dropped at the size of her *room*, which was larger than the suite at the Paris hotel. It must have spanned a third of the upstairs and was more of a mini-apartment, complete with a kitchen and dining area. Bookshelves seemed to swallow up every inch of free wall space, and each one was packed with books.

"I'm sorry it's so messy," she said, leading her around several piles of paperbacks.

"What do you do for a living?"

"Not much right now. I'm applying to doctoral programs. I'm studying to become a psychologist."

She was impressed. She had great appreciation for the study of the human mind. "That's great. Where are you hoping to go?"

"I've applied to UC San Diego, University of Washington and Arizona State. I'd like to get out of Vegas."

She led her into a dimly lit hallway in front of a large canvas. The tangle of brown drips and yellow swirls seemed to jump out at her, and for a moment she lost her breath. "This is number five."

"Yup."

She looked at her, confused. "But I heard some guy named Martinez bought this for like a hundred and forty million."

Penny shook her head with a slight smile. "Well, the price is accurate but not the buyer. That was just diversion tactics. My dad bought it and gave it to me for my birthday."

"Your dad gives great gifts," she said. "Where is your dad? Is he here?"

"No. He hates weddings. After you've been married four times the novelty wears off."

She knew little of Linus McWhirter except that he was rich and he liked young trophy wives. She suppressed the urge to ask Penny a multitude of questions about her mother and focused on the amazing work of art in front of her. Number five was one of her favorites.

They stared in silence, as if they were in church. She knew many people didn't like Pollock's work and thought his art was just a mess, but he was her favorite painter. The intricate intersections of lines and color reminded her of the human body and the freeway of arteries and capillaries buried beneath the skin's surface. She sighed deeply.

"What do you think?"

"It's unbelievable. It's so different from the reproductions I've seen. I mean, it's obviously the same painting, but it's just... so much more impressive."

She could have stared at the Pollock for another half hour, but she stepped away and smiled at Penny, well aware that they were standing in her bedroom, not a gallery.

"Thanks for showing it to me. You must look at it all the time."

She grinned. "Truthfully, I could take it or leave it." When Grace gasped, she added, "I do like it, and I like art, but my dad bought it because it was expensive, not because I wanted it."

"What *did* you want for your birthday?" she asked, stunned that anyone wouldn't want a Pollock.

"Either a nineteen twenty-eight Model A or a backpacking trip through South America."

She winced and Penny laughed. Penny took her hand and wandered to the living room. Enormous glass windows lined the east wall of the room, giving her an incredible view of the strip in the distance.

She went to a cupboard and pulled out some wineglasses. "Would you like a merlot? I noticed it seemed to be your beverage of choice."

"Um, okay."

She poured them each a glass, and they went out on the balcony and stared at the lights of Vegas. Grace could barely hear the noise from the after-party below. It seemed as though they were a hundred miles from anyone. She glanced at Penny who stared at the cityscape, content in the silence. *She's certainly not like Logan.*

"So, how long have you been into cars and motorcycles?"

"Most of my life. My dad says that was his first clue that I wasn't a girly girl."

She laughed. Her own wake-up call had been her love of Daisy Duke.

Penny glanced up, and Grace sensed small talk wasn't her forte. "So, I imagine being a surgeon is incredibly stressful. How do you go through the day knowing that people trust you one hundred percent?"

The question surprised her. Nobody had ever put it that way. "I don't know. You're right about the stress, though." She told Penny about her nightmare and her fear of losing her edge in the operating room if she expanded her social life. "I guess I'm personally doomed," she concluded.

Instead of instantly disagreeing, which was always Margo's tack, Penny didn't respond. She just swirled her wine in reflection. Eventually she said, "Then what are you doing in Vegas with Logan? Is she your girlfriend?"

"Oh, no," she said quickly. *How the hell can you explain this?* "I don't know why I'm here," she blurted.

Penny laughed and soon she laughed with her. "You know," Penny said, "maybe you've got it backwards and maybe that's why you're here. Have you ever thought the nightmare might go away if you find some balance in your personal life?"

She bit her lip. She wasn't prepared to have an intellectual conversation tonight after so much fine wine and champagne, but what Penny said made sense. She felt her eyes on her, and she suddenly wished she could fly away. *What are you afraid of, Gracie?*

"Oh, my gosh. I better go look for Logan. She's going to wonder what happened to me."

"Yeah, I'd better take you back," Penny said with little enthusiasm.

They paid homage once more to the Pollock before rejoining the party. Logan was nowhere to be found amid the drunk partygoers. Penny found Kazmar dancing with one of the naked waitresses and whispered in his ear. He pointed outside and she nodded.

Grace followed her toward a large pool house, its bright lights piercing the darkness and illuminating the vast lawn.

"I'm pretty sure I know where she is," Penny said, grinning. "C'mon."

They crossed the grass and as they approached the building, she heard a scream. She pressed her face against a huge windowpane and her jaw dropped. Splashing in the pool were Lena and Logan, both naked. They playfully chased each other until Lena allowed herself to be caught and dragged to the steps. Logan carefully set Lena above her and parted her legs. Suddenly ashamed of her peeping, Grace turned away.

"This is quite a show," Penny said, also peering through a window. "Are you surprised?"

"Not really," she lied. "But we should probably give them their privacy." She tried to pass Penny, who grabbed her by the waist and pulled her close.

"Don't go. It's okay. I know it's okay."

"What are you talking about? They're having sex. We shouldn't be watching them. It's terribly rude."

"They won't mind."

Still holding Grace in her arms, Penny stepped to the window. Logan remained between Lena's legs, and the look of pleasure on Lena's face suggested she was close to orgasm.

"Watch them. There is nothing more beautiful than two women making love, don't you agree?"

"Yes," she said, her voice barely audible.

Ten seconds later, Lena cried out and kept moaning as Logan continued to pleasure her. When their bodies finally lay still, she blinked, as if leaving a trance.

"C'mon."

Before she could protest, Penny opened the pool house door. Lena and Logan looked up, surprised. Grace prepared to heap apologies on the two women, but Lena laughed and Logan smiled broadly, which surprised her into silence.

"Can we join you?" Penny asked.

"Absolutely," Lena said, motioning to the pool. "After all, Penny, it's *your* house."

Penny disrobed immediately, but Grace remained rooted in place. She'd never skinny-dipped, and she'd never been to this type of party where anything seemed to go. Penny dove into the pool and swam to Lena. As if sensing Grace's dilemma, Logan quickly emerged from the pool and went to her.

"Grace? Are you okay?"

She nodded. "Yeah."

"Are you upset that I was with Lena?"

"No. Should I be?"

Logan smiled gently and kissed her on the cheek. "No, you shouldn't. Why don't you join us? It'll be fun. We'll give Lena a great sendoff into a life of heterosexual monogamy." She shook her head and added, "I don't think she'll make it, frankly, but hopefully Kazmar will understand."

Grace swallowed hard. "I've never done anything like this. Only my exes have seen me naked."

"Really? You didn't seem to have a problem last night."

She looked at the floor, embarrassed. "I can't really account for my actions last night."

A scream drew their attention to the pool. Penny was tickling Lena and trying to dunk her.

"Take off your clothes," Logan whispered. "Face a fear. I think that was number one on the list, wasn't it?"

She nodded at Logan and touched the side of her purse. "Is there a bathroom nearby?"

Logan pointed to a door and she left for the changing area. She dug through her purse and took a small sip from the vial. *You shouldn't need to drink too much, Grace. After all, it's just nudity. You're a doctor, for God's sake!* She closed her eyes and listened to the laughter and screams coming from the pool. She pictured all three beautiful women, naked, their bodies bathed in the glow of the moonlight seeping through the windows. Her heartbeat quickened and she held the sides of the basin. She was drawn into the river again, only this time it wasn't water rushing past her but the beautiful liquid that was the Root of Passion, caressing her body.

She managed to unzip her dress and left it in a heap on the floor. When she emerged from the changing room, Logan held out a flute of champagne.

Grace swallowed the expensive bubbly in a few sips and felt suddenly tipsy. She smiled and stepped into the pool, every nerve reacting to the cool water.

"Come play with me," Penny called from the middle. She floated on her back and kicked her legs vigorously. Grace laughed at her antics.

105

"No," Lena said, advancing toward Grace, her entire body covered by the water except her amazing face. "Do you think I'm beautiful?"

"Yes," she answered honestly.

Lena rose out of the water, and she realized they were nearly the same height. She floated into her arms, brushing against her nipples.

Lena smiled and stared at her. "Are you nervous?"

"Does it show that much?"

Lena kissed her forehead and rested her cheek against Grace's, whose legs nearly collapsed at the touch. When Lena kissed her neck, Grace relaxed in her arms.

Eventually the magic lips bit her earlobe and Lena whispered, "You know, you came to my wedding, but you didn't give me a gift."

"That's true," Grace gasped, as Lena's hands caressed her breasts. "What do you want? Some place settings from Crate and Barrel? A vase from Tiffany's?"

Lena answered by sucking on her nipples. She moaned, and Penny and Logan looked up momentarily from the other end of the pool where they were doing flips. They turned away and she felt completely alone with Lena, as if they were secluded on an isolated beach and not on display in front of two other women.

When Lena's mouth met hers again, she breathed in an incredible scent, a rich perfume she most likely could never afford.

"What are you wearing? It's amazing."

"I don't know," Lena admitted. "Whatever my dresser thought Kazmar would like."

At the mention of her husband, Grace stepped back. "Oh, my God. What are we doing?"

She looked at her sympathetically. "Come here. It's all right. Kazmar and I have no secrets. He knows I'm here. He doesn't know I'm about to claim another beautiful lesbian as a lover," she added, "but when I tell him, I'm sure he'll approve. He has great respect for doctors."

Her voice was hypnotic, her rich accent drawing Grace back into her arms. They moved in a steady rhythm and she saw the beautiful lavender liquid swirling in the vial. She moaned in pleasure, and Lena looked up.

"Am I hurting you?"

"No," she cried. "That's great."

The water swirled around them, and she saw the river swelling around the bank as her excitement grew. Hands caressed her buttocks. She opened her eyes and saw Penny standing behind Lena, kissing her neck.

"Don't stop," Logan whispered, sculpting her body against Grace's.

The four of them bobbed in the water, and she knew she was close to screaming out in joy, caught between Lena and Logan.

She visualized the Root of Passion swirling in the vial. The orgasm was like lightning, and she lost her balance. Logan caught her, and she trembled in her arms. She looked at Lena, her eyes closed, Penny cradling her against the pool deck.

Logan held her tightly. "Cross number one off your list."

Chapter Fifteen

Somewhere in Morocco

Hammers pounded in her brain, but Margo resisted the urge to open her eyes. She sensed daylight around her and the brightness gripped her skull and squeezed. She buried her head under the pillow, eliminating the light, but the hammers persisted. It took her a moment to remember she was either in Rabat or Marrakesh—she wasn't sure. This was strictly a turnaround layover and she was focused on their departure for London later that night. Morocco was merely where they'd dumped an entire contingent of wealthy oilmen, most of whom were tied to the country's royalty.

They'd taken up all of first and business class and she'd spent the entire flight feeling all thirty eyes undressing her each time she served a drink or brought a pillow. Most of them were middle-aged and gray, except for Mass. She'd learned his name much later in the evening, but their introduction had occurred minutes after the plane had departed from JFK when she'd reached over him to serve a drink to his seat companion—and felt his hand on her ass. She'd jumped slightly, but not enough to spill the drink. She glared at him and he stared back, entirely unashamed. His hand traced the curve of her buttock once more before he removed it.

He was incredibly handsome and much younger than the other men. His father was sitting two rows ahead of him, but she didn't know that at the time. Throughout the rest of the flight their eyes met constantly, and more than once Mass caught her staring at his incredible physique which was accentuated by his tailored dress shirt. He'd waited for her when she got off the plane and offered her a ride in his limousine to her hotel. She said yes to the ride and much more. He'd taken her to dinner, got her drunk, felt her up and taken her to bed.

"The universal pattern of seduction. It knows no international boundaries," she said to the pillow.

He'd departed at some point, leaving her with a splitting headache and tenderness in several intimate places. *Mass is definitely an appropriate name for him.*

Her cell phone chimed, and her hand emerged from under the pillow to search the nightstand. She flicked the phone to the floor and swore. By the time she'd retrieved it from under the bed, there was a voice mail from Grace.

She smiled as Grace rehashed the last day in an excited voice she'd never heard. The smile vanished by the time Grace described the pool orgy.

What had she done? What had Logan done? Grace certainly needed to spice up her life, but she'd crossed so many personal boundaries that Margo wondered how much therapy she'd require after she drained the vial and the Root of Passion was gone. Clearly there was some sort of drug in the potion and she was losing her mind. Would Dina ever want her, or would she scare her away?

Margo held her head in her hands, trying to think through

her hangover, realizing there was little she could do from nearly six thousand miles away. There was a seven hour time difference and since it was after eight a.m. on Sunday in Morocco that meant Grace and Logan were enjoying primetime in bed. She could call Michelle and tell her she needed to retrieve Grace, but by the time she got a flight to Sin City it would be late Sunday morning and whatever debasing activity Logan had planned would be well underway. And the likelihood of Michelle finding them would be slim.

"Hell, she'd probably join in," she muttered.

Doubts about Logan's judgment and integrity surfaced and she automatically hit Grace's cell number on her speed dial while she went to the desk and opened her laptop. After several rings, a giggling voice answered.

"Grace, is that you?"

"Hey, Margo. What's up?"

There was more laughter over a sound she didn't recognize. She heard Logan's voice but couldn't understand what she said.

"Grace, what's going on? I got your message. Is everything okay?" Grace squealed and didn't answer. "Honey, what are you doing?"

"Marg, I really can't talk right now. I'm covered in whipped cream, and Logan has made me her personal ice cream sundae."

From thousands of miles away, she distinctly heard Logan say, "I really want to eat your cherry."

She rolled her eyes and sighed. "Grace, I think we should talk. When can I call back?"

"Well, I'll be home Sunday. Or Monday," she quickly added.

"Monday? Don't you have work?"

"Yeah, but I could get Dr. Sayers to cover. He owes me. God, *everybody* in that hospital owes me for all the times I've covered for them. Poor little Grace. Always the one everyone turns to for a favor. She has no life. Let's ask Grace." She finished her speech and snorted. "I'm not worried."

But I am. "Grace, honey, I really do want to talk to you later, okay? I'm in Morocco right now and I won't be home for another four days. What I've got to say can't wait that long. When can I call you?"

But her phone had obviously fallen out of her hand, for Margo could hear her distant laughter. Grace had floated away and she wasn't sure what person had taken her place. She called her name three more times, but when Grace didn't answer, she hung up on squeals that were rapidly turning into moans.

This was all her fault. She threw on her robe and paced, glancing absently around the room. The empty pomegranate vodka bottle was responsible for the hammers in her head, and her underwear, ripped in half, lay near the doorway. Mass had wasted no time taking her to bed.

She crossed her arms and looked down. What was the difference between her and Grace? How could she sit in judgment of Grace's whipped cream delight when she'd bedded a complete stranger? Despite any concerns about Logan, Grace seemed to be having a great time. And if Logan offered Grace any drugs, she wouldn't accept them. She knew Grace would be heading to the airport—furious—not playing ice cream parlor in bed.

Remembering why she'd booted up her laptop, she typed in Logan's name and was amazed by the number of hits. Logan Brown was indeed a world-renowned photographer whose pictures were breathtaking. She admired the woman's talent as she clicked through several Google entries. Not finding much text about her, she scrolled through several pages, avoiding the photojournalistic spreads. After eight pages, almost ready to give up, she found a story about her near arrest in nineteen ninety-five. It was an AP wire story that had appeared in the *Los Angeles Times*.

According to the small blurb, she and another female passenger had been stopped by customs and questioned for several hours when she arrived in L.A. from a trip to Borneo. Apparently a baggie of herbs, roots and bark was confiscated, and only after a scientist confirmed that none of the substances constituted an illicit or illegal drug were she and her companion allowed to go. It was fishy, but it certainly wasn't a smoking gun to share with Grace. Still, it prompted her to hunt further into her past. There were three other articles about her on that page from the early nineties. She was mentioned as a constant partygoer at the swankiest clubs in New York.

She'd unwittingly clicked her way into the archives of a Manhattan gossip rag. Logan was mentioned often, her name bolded along with many other customers at the various clubs. There were a few pictures and the twenty-something Logan was a knockout, and she looked the part of the wild child, complete with skimpy miniskirt and drink in hand. There was a glassy look to her eyes, a look Margo had seen throughout her twenties in her contemporaries. Having spent time in New York, she was familiar with the club scene and she knew which ones were known for the free-flow of drugs. Eva's story seemed much more plausible to her now.

She tried a different angle and searched Root of Passion. She was surprised when several entries appeared, most of which mentioned the Valerian root and the Passion flower. She quickly learned that both were used as sedatives, and the Passion flower helped with imbalances of serotonin. She searched her memory of high school science. While she'd managed to pass Mr. Weaver's chemistry class by displaying an inappropriate amount of cleavage, she'd actually paid attention anytime the word sex had been mentioned and she remembered that serotonin levels could affect sexual drive.

She punched in Joseph's cell number, knowing he was at work in the hospital's lab.

"Hey, sweetie," he answered over several other voices. "Is this my Sex Samaritan checking up on me?"

"You know I'm always here for you if you need me. Look, I'm worried about Grace and the Root of Passion. You wouldn't believe what's going on in Vegas."

"Honestly, Margo, I doubt very much that it has anything to do with that potion."

She heard the skepticism in his voice. Whatever belief he'd had in the bar had fizzled when he stepped into the lab.

She scanned the Web page she'd pulled up. "What do you know about serotonin?"

"Serotonin? Why would you need to know about that?"

"I was doing a little research, and I'm beginning to wonder if the potion affects a person's serotonin. I mean, I can't really explain it, so that's why I'm calling you."

He sighed knowingly. "I got it. You're asking if somebody swallowed a drink, say a magic potion, and it greatly increased serotonin levels, could it alter that person's behavior?"

"Thanks. That's exactly what I'm asking. I'm glad you're fast. These international charges are killer."

"Um, well I've never heard of anything having that much power. I mean, there's been talk in the last decade about female pheromones affecting male serotonin levels and increasing sexual drive. That's obviously a straight thing, though."

"What about gay women?"

"It's funny you should mention that." She heard a door shut and imagined he'd sought out a quieter place. "There was one study done recently that suggested homosexual women and heterosexual men have similar brain responses to certain sexual chemicals."

Margo snorted. "And we all know how strongly straight guys respond to anything sexual. So, it wouldn't be beyond the realm of possibility that a lesbian's serotonin levels could be affected if she swallowed an incredible amount of pheromones?"

"Well, that's a huge jump, honey. I've never heard of any chemical that had that sort of effect."

"What about something natural, like a root?"

"Ah, I see. Well, there are some herbs and roots that are supposed to be linked to pheromones in other animals, but we're not talking about humans. I've only heard of the perfume they've tried to make from some different types of pheromones. I think you're climbing up a ridiculous tree here, and you're freaking me out. We never talk about this stuff. I'm the scientist, and I'm telling you to let it go. Your mystery shop was probably a joke shop. Okay?"

She sighed. "Okay. I've gotta go, honey."

She hung up, her mind swirling. Could the mysterious Root of Passion be controlling Grace's sexual drive? She pictured her best friend slathered in whipped cream, an image that she couldn't have fathomed a week ago. She thought of innocent Grace and worldly Logan, a woman with a racy past, a woman that Grace barely knew, spending another day in one of the raunchiest cities in America.

Chapter Sixteen

Grace rolled over, realizing she was alone in bed. The smell of coffee and waffles filled her senses. Logan must have risen and ordered breakfast, leaving her to sleep. And she definitely needed more sleep. They'd spent much of the night doing things that she'd only seen in porn flicks, and when she thought of her behavior, her face flushed. The clock read ten thirty, prompting her to chuckle. The last time she'd slept past nine was two years before, when a surgery ran nearly to midnight.

Her brain switched into work mode and she thought of her patients suffering in their hospital beds while she behaved like a complete hedonist. She knew Dr. Van Buren was an excellent physician but guilt curled up next to her, and she wondered if she shouldn't go back to Phoenix immediately. She thought of Chester, her most elderly patient. He could take a nosedive at any time for any reason simply because of his age. How would Logan feel if her father died while she was pleasuring his doctor? She wasn't sure if she could forgive herself if something happened. Acknowledging that her career was the most important part of her life, she rose from the bed with purpose and went to find Logan. She needed to be home that evening.

She found her lounging on the sofa, reading the newspaper. She wore one of the hotel robes, but she'd haphazardly cinched the belt, and the robe covered very little. She swallowed hard and thought about their bodies colliding throughout the night. The sex was amazing, and disappointment washed over her as she realized they wouldn't spend another evening together. Logan smiled seductively at Grace, who hadn't bothered to put on anything. "Are you up for more?" she asked, dropping the paper to her lap. "I'm all for morning sex."

She shook her head and perched on the sofa's arm. "I don't think I could handle another round. You wore me out."

Logan arched an eyebrow. "Really? I thought you did a great job keeping up."

She pulled Grace onto the sofa and her lips immediately landed in the hollow of her neck. *How did she learn about my erogenous zones so quickly?*

Determined to stay focused, Grace said, "I think I need to get back tonight. I'm a little concerned about my patients, including your father."

Her playfulness vanished and she looked at her seriously. "Why are you suddenly worried? Did Dr. Van Buren call? Is there a problem?"

"No," she said quickly. "It's just that I don't leave my patients very often and I worry about them."

Logan sighed and kissed her on the cheek. "You're so attentive, but you're also a workaholic and that's not good. You need to live your life, Grace. You need to have fun and take risks."

"I think I've been doing a fine job of that for the last twenty-four hours."

"I agree. But you've only been gone a *day* and you're ready to go home. What happens when you take a vacation, like a cruise or a week long walking tour through Wales?"

She shrugged. She couldn't remember the last time she'd taken a real vacation. Until Logan had entered her life, she couldn't think of anyone she wanted to vacation with. Margo would have been happy to pack her bags in a minute, but the idea of traveling with Margo scared her.

She ignored Logan's question and headed toward the breakfast fare that sat on the dining table. Logan had ordered six different entrées, and after she'd gone back to the bedroom and slipped on the teddy, she planted herself in front of the overflowing plates, her mouth already watering. Logan eventually joined her and they ate in silence. *At least she knows when to let a subject drop*, she thought. She savored the crêpes, gorged on the French toast and drank four cups of the most delicious coffee she'd ever tasted.

"It's good, isn't it?" Logan asked, and she nodded. "I like the way you dress for breakfast, too."

She smiled and noticed that her tiny spaghetti straps had dropped from her shoulders, revealing the curves of her breasts. The prim and proper Grace would have quickly readjusted her clothing, embarrassed by her overt display of sexuality—even in the presence of a lover. But this new Grace, the one who had apparently hijacked the old one in Phoenix, continued to nibble on her waffle while Logan's eyes feasted on her bare skin. At one point Grace leaned back and propped her feet up on the nearby chair, spreading her legs and giving Logan a clear view. *An area she's certainly becoming quite familiar with.*

Eventually Logan dropped her fork on the china plate and grabbed her hand. They went back to the bedroom until early afternoon. The phone rang just as she warmed to the idea of spending the entire day in bed, something she'd never done in her life. The soft sheets cocooned her in the most pleasant way. *I have no desire to get dressed. I want to stay naked.*

"That was Penny," Logan said after she hung up. "She wants us at the estate in an hour. Then we'll go riding."

She shook her head. She'd changed her mind about riding on

a motorcycle, even with a helmet. *At least I've had one clear vision.* "I'm not going. You can if you want but I'm not getting on that death machine."

"Death machine? C'mon, Grace. You'll love it, and it'll help you cross number one off your list."

"I *already* crossed number one off my list. That happened in the pool. Remember?"

Logan chuckled and snuggled against her. "Look, you'll really enjoy it. And you still have two more items to go." She reached across the bed and plucked the list from the nightstand. "According to this, you need to wear something sexy and make a public spectacle of yourself."

Grace grabbed the paper and threw it on the floor. "As far as I'm concerned, I've finished the list. I've never worn anything as sexy as this teddy you bought me and I'm rather certain that having sex in a pool with a stranger counts as a public spectacle."

"Oh, no," Logan disagreed. "You can't do a two for one. I know your friend Margo would agree with me."

"Well, Margo's not here, and I make the rules. I'm not getting on a motorcycle. Margo will have to be disappointed."

As the cab pulled up to the McWhirter estate, Grace realized it was probably a mistake to let Logan talk her into leaving the hotel. While she had no intention of straddling a hog, Logan and Penny had coaxed her into spending the day by the pool while they motored across the highways outside of Vegas. Penny had assured her that she owned a swimsuit that would fit her slim frame, and she'd grudgingly agreed because she didn't want to spend the day alone in an isolated hotel room. At least at the estate she could stroll about the grounds and reflect on her past behavior. *And you've got a lot to think about, Gracie.*

They wandered into the garage and found Penny dressed in tight jeans and a black T-shirt.

"You look fabulous," Logan said, enfolding Penny in her arms and kissing her cheek.

"You're pretty hot yourself, gorgeous," she replied.

Dressed in jeans, a tank top and a leather jacket, Logan looked equally attractive. A twinge of jealousy surged through Grace, who couldn't believe the woman she'd fondled and sucked for the past twelve hours was openly flirting with someone else. *Let it go. They're spending the rest of the day together. They'll probably ride for an hour and get a hotel room on the strip. It doesn't matter.*

Penny grinned at her. "Change your mind?"

"Nope."

"Let me show you something," Penny said, taking her hand and leading her to the row of motorcycles against the wall.

Two of the newer models had been brought from the line and she assumed Penny had chosen them for the afternoon's ride. Her gaze fell on the shiny chrome immediately and the studded saddlebags of the bike to her right.

Penny stroked the seat. "It's a nineteen ninety-seven Harley Softail Classic. It looks old-fashioned, but it's not."

"Cool," Logan said. "How does it ride?"

"Smooth. It's quiet, and it's got the rear suspension. That's why they call it a softail."

She patted the small second seat perched over the back wheel. "This would be your spot, Grace. You'd be able to see everything."

"I don't think so. I'll stay here and enjoy the pool."

"Um, that's not going to work." She lowered her eyes, a guilty expression on her face. "The pool's being resurfaced. Sorry. They just started this morning."

"On *Sunday*?" Grace asked suspiciously.

Penny shrugged. "What can I say? When Linus McWhirter wants something done, it happens. I'm sorry. They just showed up."

She frowned. Penny didn't look sorry at all. She glanced at the tiny seat, wondering how she would ever stay upright. She pictured herself clinging to Penny, her arms clutching her middle. She was stuck.

"Don't worry, Grace," Logan said. "I've ridden my whole life. It's perfectly safe. You can ride with me if you want."

Her gaze immediately shifted to Penny, who looked away. She shook her head and sighed. "No, if I'm going to do this I'll need to ride with the expert."

Penny grinned broadly and her eyes probed Grace's body. "You're gonna need a different outfit. I can help you with that."

She glanced down at the beautiful silk blouse and linen pants she wore. She looked fabulous but it didn't matter. She longed to return to the hotel but it was thirty minutes away, and she couldn't ask Logan and Penny to take her back.

"Let's get you dressed," Penny said, taking her hand and leading her through the house to the familiar spiral staircase.

Her eyes lingered on the Pollock as they headed into Penny's vast bedroom.

"I know exactly what you need," Penny said, throwing open her walk-in closet. She disappeared and returned with a pair of jeans, a Harley-Davidson tank top and riding boots.

"These are my old pair, but your feet look like they'll fit."

She accepted the pile of clothing and looked for the bathroom. "Where can I change?"

"Why not right here?" Logan asked seductively. They fell onto Penny's bed to watch, lewd smiles on their faces. "Honey, it's not like we haven't seen you in the buff."

Her gaze settled on what she thought was the bathroom door and she headed in that direction.

"You're no fun," Penny called after her.

The bathroom was immense, complete with dressing area, Jacuzzi tub and twin sinks. She changed quickly, thinking that the longer Penny and Logan were alone the more likely it was they would start having sex—and then expect her to join them.

She found a full-length mirror inside the bathroom door and appraised herself with a critical eye. Everything fit snugly, and she estimated Penny was a size smaller than she. The jeans hugged her like a second skin and the waistband sat far beneath her belly button, almost to her pubic bone. She'd never worn such low-cut pants. She removed her bra since its lavender straps looked tacky underneath the spaghetti strings that held up the tank top. The Harley-Davidson logo spread across her chest in sequins, exposing deep cleavage and much of her midriff. She hoped Penny had a jacket to wear over the tiny top or everyone would see her bouncing boobs. She pulled out the comb in her hair and struck a pose with her hands in the jeans' back pockets. *Maybe I do look hot.*

She reached into her purse and pulled out the vial. A quick dose of Root of Passion, and she felt ready for anything. The vial was almost empty and she wondered when Margo would return to South America. She leaned against the wall, laced her fingers behind her head and closed her eyes for a few seconds, allowing the river to rush past her once more. When she blinked, the woman in the mirror was someone she didn't know. She checked out her backside, pleased at the way the jeans hugged her bottom.

She found Logan and Penny still lounging on the bed, whispering to each other. They whistled and hooted as she crossed the room, and Penny leaped up and yanked her onto the bed with them.

"Let's just stay here and have a threesome," she said.

Logan stared at her and she found she couldn't take her eyes away. She suddenly wished they were alone, free of Penny and the commitment to go riding.

"You are absolutely hot," Penny said. "What do you think, Logan?"

"I agree," she answered. "I think you can cross off number four. This outfit definitely has sex appeal."

Grace's face immediately reddened.

Logan jumped up and headed for the door. "Let's ride."

Chapter Seventeen

Thanks to the Root of Passion, Grace had no problem straddling the motorcycle and wrapping her arms around Penny's waist. Within thirty minutes they'd roared into the Spring Mountain Range, heading up Mt. Charleston's summit road. As they ascended, the line of Joshua trees gave way to clusters of cedars. Penny had mentioned that at the top of the mountain was an Alpine forest. The wind whipped past Grace's face and she was grateful for the soft leather jacket Penny had found before they left the garage. Her hands remained glued to Penny's side, but gone were the visions of the bike skittering into a ditch or the image of her crushed skull after they kissed the side of a mountain. *This is what it's like to be free.*

They stopped twice, once to look at a wild burro and once to admire the view below them before they started back down. She gazed out at the valley, locating the road they'd just traveled, a tiny artery that cut through the mountain. She breathed deeply, the clean air filling her lungs. She pictured the dirty air she sucked in each morning during her run. She'd rarely ventured into nature and she suddenly felt deprived.

"You look mesmerized," Logan said.

"I don't get out much," she replied. "Maybe I should."

"There's nothing like camping," Penny added, returning her water bottle to the saddlebag. "My ex and I used to come up here two or three times a year. There are some great spots."

"I've never camped," she said.

Logan threw her leg over the bike and prepared to ride. "You're right, Grace. You need to get out more."

Penny arched her eyebrows and revved the engine. "Let's go, Grace. We'll zip back down and have some *real* fun."

She wondered what else could be in store for her. She was at Penny's mercy and didn't care. She rested her chin on Penny's shoulder, staring at the white lines that zipped past them at lightning speed. The bike twisted right and left, the surrounding mountain wall just a few feet away. She could almost reach over and touch the granite surface. It seemed much more real than when she traveled in an enclosed car. She thought of the trip she made each fall, traveling on Highway 89A between Prescott and Jerome in Arizona, marveling at the changing leaves. Now she realized how much more enjoyable the ride would be free of the metal and glass separating her from nature. There could be no comparison.

The rumble of the motor vibrated between her legs and her thoughts immediately turned sexual. She glanced over at Logan, who was alternating her gaze between the road and Grace. She grinned, and Grace realized how sexy she looked on the Harley. *What would it be like to make love on a motorcycle? Was that possible?*

She laughed, knowing that a few days before she never would have had such thoughts. When she read her lesbian romances she blushed at the sex parts. How could those writers think of such things? And now she was having fantasies worthy of Karin

Kallmaker and Radclyffe. *Think about it, Grace. In the last two days, you've made love to two different women—a famous photographer and a famous model—you've attended <u>the</u> wedding of the year and you've ridden a motorcycle.* She realized she was either going insane or waking up from a lifetime of deadness.

She was sorry to see the sign announcing their exit from the mountain range. Penny sailed down the highway for several miles before motioning at Logan to turn right. Grace saw a road ahead, one she hadn't noticed during their ride to the mountain. They made the turn and rode down a long straightaway, the rich, lush landscape quickly fizzling into desert brush. Traveling amid the tans and browns wasn't as appealing as the mountain roads and she found herself longing to reach the destination. Her ass was killing her.

The scenery seemed to repeat—tumbleweeds and dust endlessly appearing in front of them. It was hypnotic and her eyelids slowly closed. She blinked awake as they were approaching a large green sign. She read the scripted letters: Serendipity. Penny slowed the bike as the speed limit commanded her to do, and they chugged into the outskirts of the tiny town. They passed a series of closed businesses—gas station, Laundromat and mini-mart. The scene reminded her of every poor small town she'd ever driven through—a dot on the map, gasping to stay alive. *This doesn't seem serendipitous to me.*

She wondered why Penny would want them to come this way—until she saw the glint of chrome in the distance.

Through the swirling dust she recognized rows of motorcycles lined up in front of a building that looked like a huge metal shed. The word Hardbelly's flashed in neon lights above the door and rock music filled the parking lot.

Penny parked next to a monstrous cycle twice the size of the Softail. A rugged middle-aged biker and his motorcycle mama were checking their storage compartments, and they both took a long look at Grace when Penny pulled up. Logan roared up beside them and parked her bike.

"Give me the jacket," Penny said. "You won't need it inside."

Grace obliged, feeling incredibly exposed in front of the man and woman who made no effort to avert their gaze. She could only imagine how she looked as she removed her helmet and handed it to Penny. Her hair was a mess and she shook it out, drawing a smile from her audience.

"Hey, quit staring," Penny said to the couple. "Haven't you ever seen a totally hot biker chick?"

Grinning, the bikers turned away obediently, and Penny wrapped an arm around her bare midriff. *I'm almost topless*, she thought.

"What is this place?" Logan asked.

"This is the best biker bar within a hundred miles." Penny pulled Grace against her and kissed her neck. "It's my turn to have you."

She automatically glanced at Logan, who seemed not to notice. Her gaze was focused on the bar. "Are you sure this kind of place appreciates diversity?"

Penny laughed and led them inside. A long bar lined the back and cocktail tables dotted most of the space. Harley-Davidson paraphernalia covered the walls and an antique motorcycle hung in the far corner, suspended by several chains. Shouts erupted from the bar and she saw the plasma TV televising a football game. Across from the bar was a small stage, a microphone stand in the center.

The place was packed. She was rather certain the PETA people would be quite displeased with the vast amount of leather that covered every biker's body. Depending on where she turned her gaze, her every biker stereotype was confirmed or denied. Long-haired, mutton-chopped bikers wearing faded and tattered denim jackets and Levi's shared space with clean-cut, fashionable, respectable types who she guessed only rode on the weekends. She'd read about the weekend bikers—accountants, lawyers and CEOs whose secret passion was riding. As her gaze flitted around the bar she found the idea surprisingly appealing, particularly when she saw two different lesbian couples openly making out. *Your mother would have heart failure, Gracie.*

Logan tried to say something to her but gave up, unable to compete with Bruce Springsteen's bellowing and the noise of the boisterous patrons talking over the music. It was the loudest bar she'd ever entered, and no one seemed to realize or care that they were shouting to their neighbor.

Penny pulled her close and said in her ear, "You guys go find a table and I'll get us some drinks."

She nodded and took Logan's hand. As they wormed their way through the tables, she tried not to stare at the variety of characters that huddled together. Her gaze wandered to a giant man, his forearms covered in skull tattoos and an enormous gauge in each ear. She saw the stage through the hole in his lobe and she couldn't imagine how painful that procedure must be. When he stared back, her cheeks reddened. Logan caught her arm and propelled her in another direction, toward a table where a group of bikers was preparing to leave.

When they'd settled on the stools, Logan shouted, "So what do you think of this place?"

"This is definitely a new experience for me. Don't you dare disappear," she added.

Logan leaned over for a quick kiss. "I won't. I'll be right here. And there's something else I want to say."

"What?"

"I don't want you to be with Penny. I know she's planning to make a move on you."

She smiled, extremely pleased. *Is Logan falling for me?* "I don't want to be with Penny. I only want you."

She touched Logan's cheek and soon they were kissing passionately. The sound of clinking glass pulled them apart. Penny stood there, holding a tray of tequila shooters.

"Am I interrupting something?"

There was no mistaking her acid tone and she felt obliged to explain, but Logan said, "C'mon, Penny. Don't be mad. We're here to have fun, right? I can't help that Grace is mesmerized by my overwhelming charms."

She snorted and rolled her eyes. They both looked at Penny,

whose expression showed resignation to the situation.

"Okay, I'll accept that I'm the third wheel, but if we're gonna have fun then let's play a game."

It was nearly six. "How long will it take to get back to the hotel?" she asked Logan.

Logan and Penny exchanged knowing glances. Penny leaned over and said into her ear, "You're not going back to the hotel tonight. By the time we get back to my house it'll be really late. I thought we could have a slumber party."

She sat up straight and shook her head. "No, I need to check on my patients."

"Grace, they're fine, at least my dad is. When we stopped earlier I called my sister. He's had a good weekend and Dr. Van Buren saw him twice. You don't need to worry. You're on vacation. One more night isn't going to make a difference."

"I don't believe this. You're kidnapping me."

Logan's hand, which had rested on her back, slid downward and Grace jumped slightly. "Don't you want another night of hot sex?" she cooed into her ear.

She laughed and kissed her. "Okay, what game are we playing?" she asked Penny. "Penny?"

Hearing her name, Penny turned back to the table. She'd been eyeing the bar, and when Grace looked in the same direction, she noticed a statuesque brunette in a tight jumpsuit.

Definitely hotter than me.

Penny thought for a moment. "Let's play, I Never."

"How do you play?" she asked, feeling incredibly sheltered. "I'm not up on many drinking games."

"It's really easy," Logan explained. "Somebody makes a true statement that starts with the words, I never. Then, if anyone else has done what the statement says, you have to drink."

"I'll go first," Penny said. "I've never been to jail."

Having never been arrested, Grace just smiled, but she was rather surprised when Logan said, "Shit," and hoisted one of the shooters to her lips.

After Logan smacked the shot glass on the table, she asked

her, "You went to jail? For what?"

"No, no," Penny said. "That's also one of the rules. The drinker doesn't have to explain herself."

"My turn," Logan said. "I never…" Her voice faded away and she shook her head. "There's not a lot to choose from." She drummed her fingers on the table for a moment and looked up grinning. "I never kept a girlfriend for longer than six months."

Grace and Penny glanced at each other and reached for a shooter. The tequila burned going down, and she gasped for breath.

"A little strong, huh?" Penny joked. "Your turn, Grace."

"Um, I've never been to Australia."

Both Penny and Logan groaned as they reached for a drink. She had deduced that the point was to get the other participants drunk while maintaining her own sobriety. Considering how boring her life was, she was rather certain she could win.

Penny eyed her shrewdly. "I've never worn a skirt to work."

She reached for another shooter but noticed Logan shaking her head. *Of course she wouldn't wear a skirt.* The second shooter went down smoothly, and she felt slightly lightheaded.

"Okay," Logan said, "I've never been to an NFL football game."

"You haven't?" Penny asked incredulously. "How can that be?"

Logan shrugged while Penny and Grace picked their shooters. "I grew up in Phoenix and we didn't have a team for a long time. And I've just never had an interest in watching sweaty men jump all over each other."

"My turn," Grace said in a loud voice. "I've never used cocaine."

"Christ, Grace, you're killing me," Penny growled. She and Logan downed a shot.

There were still six glasses left on the tray. She wondered how many more she could handle before she fell off the stool.

"I've never kept a journal," Penny said.

She thought of the leopard-spotted book she hid under her

bed all through junior high. She'd written all about her girlhood crushes as she came to terms with her lesbianism.

"Grace, are you telling me you never kept a journal? You?" Penny asked.

"Oh, sorry." She threw her head back and the tequila coated her throat nicely.

Logan folded her hands on the table. "I've never karaoked."

Penny reached for a glass and glanced at her. "You haven't karaoked?"

She shook her head. "Me? Are you crazy? I can't sing very well to begin with. I'm certainly not going to sing in public."

Logan laughed. "Oh, yes, you are."

"What?"

Logan pointed to a spot over her shoulder. When she turned, she saw the enormous sign next to the stage announcing that Sunday was karaoke night, starting at seven thirty.

"No way," she said. "I'm not doing that."

"You'll finish the list—well, almost."

She suddenly remembered. *Make a public spectacle of yourself.* That would certainly qualify, but she'd sooner be bitten by a tarantula than sing in public.

"No."

"What list?" Penny asked.

"Grace's friends made this list of things for her to do, and she's crossed everything off, except making a public spectacle of herself and having a relationship."

Penny's arms encircled her bare waist and she stroked her belly. "You should do it."

She closed her eyes, enjoying Penny's touch. Eva used to love kissing her belly on her way down to the sweet spot between her legs. Lost in her thoughts, she hardly noticed Penny's hand groping her breast.

Her eyes shot open and she stared at Logan, who was watching the entire scene, an empty shot glass in her hand. Apparently the game was over.

"Somebody's a little drunk," Logan said, frowning.

She pushed Penny's hand away. "I need to hit the bathroom."

She hopped off the stool and headed toward the bar, unsure of where to go but wanting to be away from both of the women. Penny's touch was too tempting and Logan's stare chilled her instantly.

Once she'd found the bathroom she went to the sink and pulled the list from her purse. She glanced at the tiny top and low-cut jeans, realizing that she'd never dressed so sexually. She reapplied her lipstick and stared critically at the woman who stared back. Her deep red lips added to the effect, but it wasn't enough. *You look like you're trying and failing.* She dug through her purse and found the makeup pouch she'd added to her purchases at the Paris shop. The eyeliner was a rich black, and she liberally applied it to her eyes. *Now it all matches.* She brushed her hair quickly and washed her hands. She put everything away and held the list. Yes, Logan was correct and only one item remained that she could accomplish this weekend. *But maybe not! Maybe Logan will want a relationship.* She pulled the vial from her purse and drank. Only a few drops remained.

She carefully put the box back in her bag and returned to the table, stumbling slightly as she walked. She was definitely buzzed and only a step away from drunk. *Who cares? You're not driving.* The shots were gone, except for one that sat in front of her stool. Penny was also missing.

"This one's for you," Logan said.

She hesitated only for a second, already thinking of the Root of Passion coursing through her system. She downed the shot, and the room spun. She planted her hands on the table for support. Penny appeared, carrying a tray of beers. Following close behind her was the brunette in the jumpsuit. Grace's eyes probed the woman's body and it was impossible to miss her strategic cleavage, since she'd zipped the jumpsuit just high enough to meet public decency laws. She realized that the zipper disappeared between her legs. *Talk about easy access.*

"Time for a new game," Penny said, setting the beers in the

middle of the table. "Oh, and this is Cady. We met at the bar."

"Hey," Cady offered, flashing the whitest teeth she'd ever seen. *Definitely bleached.*

"So what's the game?" Logan asked, resting her hand on Grace's leg.

Now that Penny had found a new playmate, Logan had no problem reminding her of their incredible chemistry. The Root of Passion had to be working, counteracting the effects of the alcohol. She felt clear and free, just as she had the night in the restaurant with Michelle.

"Let's play Beer Race." Penny looked at her to explain. "This one's simple. We each take a beer and when I say go, we chug the beer. The first person who finishes holds her empty mug upside down over her head."

Cady laughed and added, "Then everybody else has to do the same, no matter how much beer is left in your mug."

"This could get really messy," Grace said.

"Have you seen the floor of this place?" Penny asked.

She glanced down at the concrete. She hadn't noticed that spilled drinks were everywhere. The management obviously didn't care and saw it as a moneymaker.

Penny set a beer in front of each of them. "Go!"

She drank as fast as she could, but it was apparent everyone else was highly experienced at beer chugging. Cady finished first and held the mug over her head.

"I win!"

Both Penny and Logan were nearly finished, so when they poured the beer over their heads, very little dribbled down their faces. They all laughed and everyone stared at Grace, whose beer mug was still half full. She giggled and turned it over her head, closing her eyes and jumping slightly when the cold liquid dripped between her breasts. It felt wonderful.

"Again!" Penny commanded. "Go!"

This time Penny drained her mug first, but Logan and Cady were close behind. Only Grace found herself again drenched in beer.

Logan whispered, "This is starting to turn into a wet T-shirt contest, and I am *so* enjoying it."

She glanced down at her top. It was covered in beer and her nipples stood erect. She saw the lust in Logan's eyes and without thinking another thought, she reached for her last beer and poured it over her head. The other three women applauded, and she laughed until she cried.

At some point Logan started kissing her, and Penny and Cady were forgotten. The Root of Passion held her, and her whole body responded.

"How long will it take us to get back to the hotel?" she groaned.

Logan laughed and cradled her chin. "Oh, no. You're not leaving until you karaoke. You want to make love? Then you'll sing for your sex, lady."

She shook her head. "I don't think so. I'm in no shape to stand on a stage in front of a crowd. Look at me." They both glanced down at her tank top, plastered to her skin.

"You look hot," Logan said.

Suddenly the bar went dark and a spotlight appeared on the stage. "Ladies and gentlemen, it's karaoke night at Hardbelly's!"

The crowd roared its approval, and a cute redhead wearing jeans and a cowboy shirt jumped on the stage. The crowd screamed as she grabbed the microphone. "Hey ya'll. How's everyone doin' tonight?" The crowd responded with cheers and she waited patiently. "Well, tonight's our weekly karaoke and I've been told that we have a special performance in store for us from a woman who's probably the most educated person ever to set foot on the Hardbelly's stage."

She turned to Logan. "No."

Logan only grinned as the woman shouted into the microphone, "Please give a great Hardbelly's welcome to Dr. Grace Owens!"

All she heard were the cheers, but she remained planted on her chair until Logan, Penny and Cady literally carried her to the stage. They stepped away and the cute redhead took her arm.

She noted that the woman's grip was like a vise as she planted her center stage.

When the crowd quieted, the redhead asked, "Now, what are you going to sing for us, Grace?"

"I don't sing," she said weakly, and the crowd laughed hysterically.

She wanted to disappear, but the redhead's fingers were firmly clamped around her upper arm. She wasn't going anywhere. This woman was tough. *She probably rides bulls or brands cattle for a living.*

"Now, Grace, everybody karaokes. You really don't have to sing." When she remained mute, the woman added, "Your friends told me this might happen, so they picked a song for you."

"I really can't do this," she pleaded.

"Of course you can." The woman turned to the audience. "Let's give Grace our full support. C'mon, ya'll!"

The crowd chanted, "Grace! Grace! Grace!" and Grace, through the blinding spotlight, managed to see a few of the excited faces.

Suddenly the music started and the redhead pointed to a nearby screen. She saw the words for Willie Nelson's *On the Road Again* appear, and the redhead dragged her through the first verse. Her eyes remained glued to the monitor, watching the words appear and erase.

By the second verse, her confidence soared, and she realized that the redhead had released her death grip and in fact was standing in a corner, clapping along with the crowd. She was on her own. Elated, she glanced at the monitor, but she knew the song. It was one of her mother's favorites and she'd heard it a million times. She took a few steps toward the crowd, belting the lyrics, and a huge flash erupted which she imagined was Logan's camera. The whoops and hoots grew, drowning out her horrible singing. She returned to the chorus and pranced across the stage, shaking her breasts at the drunken patrons. The response was deafening and gave her the courage to perform the final verse. She swayed back and forth, grinding her hips to the music, until

133

the song ended.

The redhead rushed to her side and presented her to the crowd: "Grace Owens!"

She took a bow and waved at the cheering crowd. *I feel like a rock star.* The grin across her face matched the exhilaration in her heart. As she returned to her seat people clapped, shouted her name and patted her on the back. She was one of them. She'd never felt so comfortable around complete strangers. *You hate crowds, remember?*

Logan threw her arms around her. "I'm so proud of you. You've almost finished the list." She stepped back and held her shoulders. "I guess my work here is done. We can go home."

She swallowed hard. She suddenly wished they weren't going home. *I want to feel this way forever.*

"Are you okay, Grace?" Logan asked, touching her cheek.

She glanced back toward the stage, avoiding her concerned stare. The patrons were focused on the next singer who belted out *Crazy.*

Now she's really good. Logan's arms enveloped her, and they got up and swayed to the slow song. *I am crazy for Logan, but it could never work. She said so.*

The next performer was worse than Grace, but the drunk crowd cheered, although less enthusiastically than they did for her. *But she isn't wearing a tank top covered in beer.* They stayed for another hour, until Penny and Logan felt sober enough to drive.

Cady claimed Penny's second seat which pleased Grace immensely. She snuggled against Logan without feeling guilty about Penny's affections. *Penny won't have any trouble unzipping that jumpsuit.*

They returned to the main road and headed back toward the lights of Las Vegas. She couldn't imagine how she'd ever thought it was a terrible place. She realized she'd made the same assumptions about many places—and many people. Eva had tried to introduce her to new things, new friends and new experiences. She'd always balked, using work as an excuse.

Before she could control herself, her cheeks were wet. She didn't dare move her hands away from Logan's waist, so the tears dried on her face, a reminder of her pain. She vowed to call Eva and apologize when she got home. She owed her that much. She couldn't have been much of a girlfriend. *I'll be different next time. Maybe there'll be something between me and Logan.*

Chapter Eighteen

When they roared through the McWhirter front gate, a compact car was parked in the circle drive by the massive front door. The night was black and she couldn't see the figure pacing outside the garage's entrance until the motorcycle's headlight shone directly on her—Eva. *What the hell?*

Both Penny and Logan stopped their bikes, and they all dismounted. Eva ran to Grace and threw her arms around her.

"Honey, are you okay?"

She pried Eva's arms from her shoulders and pulled her helmet off. Eva blinked in surprise, and she imagined that she was quite a sight in her smudged makeup.

"Eva, why are you here?"

"I was worried about you." She glanced at the other three women and said, "Can we talk privately?"

Penny took a step toward Eva. "Friend of yours, Grace?"

"My ex. It's okay." She took her arm and led her toward the house. "So, answer my question. Why are you here?"

"What I said was true. I'm worried about you. When Margo mentioned—"

"Margo? What does Margo have to do with this? Did she send you here? I can't believe it!"

"She didn't send me. She doesn't know I came to Vegas. All she did was tell me that you'd come here with Logan, and then I got really worried."

She shook her head and scowled. "Why? Because I might finally have a little fun? I might've actually met someone who helped me come out of my shell?"

Eva frowned. "Oh, she helped you all right. I can see that just from your attire. Would you like to know how she *helped* you?"

"What are you talking about?"

Eva didn't answer. Instead she unzipped Grace's jacket, exposing her still mostly wet T-shirt. Her eyes widened. "My God. Did you go out in public like this?"

"Yes," she said, slipping the jacket off and letting Eva have a good look at her sexy attire. "And I sang karaoke," she added proudly.

Eva shook her head. "Gracie." Tears pooled in her eyes, and she cupped her chin. "Think about it. How did she get you to do that? How did she get you to dress like this? This isn't you. What did she give you?"

She looked away, unwilling to divulge the secret of the Root of Passion. "She didn't give me anything."

"Oh, yes she did," Eva said, her voice cracking. Grace could tell she was crying. "I wasn't sure until now, but looking at you..." Her voice trailed off, and she stepped away. "She gave you E, Grace. I know it."

"No, Eva, she didn't. Logan would never do that. I know you're jealous. We may have something here, something special." She found herself smiling, and, despite Eva's pain, she couldn't control the excitement in her voice. "It's been an unbelievable

137

two days—"

"I saw her buy the drugs. She got them in Phoenix at the hospital."

The idea slammed into her and made her wobble. *She has to be mistaken. She's just jealous. She's saying things to hurt me and slander Logan because she wants me back.*

"I don't believe you. You're either wrong or you're lying. I'm just not sure which it is."

Eva held her shoulders and gazed into her eyes. "Grace, this is *me*, Eva. I've got the eagle eyes, remember? I'm the one with twenty-ten vision. And I've never lied to you."

She pulled away. "No, you didn't lie. You just didn't tell me everything I needed to know, like how boring I was."

Eva's gaze dropped to the ground. "There was no point, Grace. You are who you are. I just had to accept that we were too different. I'd never say anything that hurtful to you." She looked up again, tears streaming down her face. "I love you too much."

"Grace?"

Both of them looked over Grace's shoulder at Logan, who appeared at her side, slipping her arm around her waist. "You okay, baby?"

She glanced at Eva, wiping the tears from her face, clearly embarrassed. "Why don't you ask her, Grace? Just ask her. If I'm wrong I'll get out of here, you all can have a good laugh and fuck the night away."

Logan grinned at her. "Now that sounds like a good way to end the evening. What do you need to ask me?"

"Since we've been on this trip, have you slipped me some E?"

For a split second, Logan's grin cracked, but she quickly recovered. "What?"

She watched her face, focusing on her eyes. Years of working with patients and their families had taught her that people lied all the time, even when faced with life-and-death situations. She'd learned to read people to save their lives. The crack in Logan's smile sent a wave of doubt through her. She'd known her for two days and Eva for many years. She pulled out of her embrace and crossed her arms.

"I'm asking if you gave me any narcotics without my knowledge."

Logan held her stare, and she waited for her to look away. It would be a sure sign of her guilt. *Please don't. Please let Eva be wrong.*

When Logan blinked and shifted her gaze to Eva, Grace's heart sank. Logan raked her hand through her hair nervously and started pacing. "Look, I'm sorry I didn't tell you, but you were so uptight, and I knew that if I could just loosen you up, help you check off everything on that list, you'd gain some self-esteem."

She couldn't believe what she was hearing. "Self-esteem? You gave me an illegal drug—one that can cause kidney and liver failure—because you thought my self-image needed a boost? I can't believe this!" She knew she was shouting, but she couldn't help it. "I'm a doctor, for God's sake! Did you ever stop to think that you could ruin my career?"

Logan rolled her eyes. "Grace, you need to calm down. A couple little trips on E aren't going to make you an addict, and it isn't going to fry your system."

Her jaw dropped. "A *couple* trips? How many times did you give it to me?"

Realizing her mistake, Logan bit her lip before she answered. "Twice. The first time I slipped it in the champagne I gave you at the pool house, and then I dropped a pill into your shooter tonight."

"It's still in my system? Right now?"

"How long ago did you drink the shooter, Grace?" Eva asked.

She turned to Eva, whose face was full of concern. "About four hours ago."

"Then the main effects have passed, but you should probably drink lots of water to avoid dehydration."

She suddenly realized how parched her throat was, and she'd

assumed it was from the alcohol. She glanced back at Logan whose expression conveyed nothing—no remorse, no anger, no sadness. *This was just another ride to her.* She wanted to go home. She wanted to cry. She wanted to be as far away from Logan as possible. Before the stream of tears could come, Eva took her arm and led her away.

Chapter Nineteen

Grace caught the elevator just before the steel doors groaned shut. It was almost eleven and she'd completed her rounds, including an uncomfortable twenty minutes with Chester Brown who wanted to quiz her about the weekend. She summoned every ounce of professionalism she possessed and dodged his personal questions with humor and patience. Fortunately, he'd be released later in the day.

She headed for the basement and the tunnel that led to the staff parking garage elevator. Most doctors chose to travel the passage, avoiding the possibility of a confrontation with a patient's inquisitive family or a call from a colleague for an impromptu consult. She rarely entered or exited the hospital this way, enjoying the opportunity to visit with other doctors and nurses in the hospital. Today, though, she wanted out, and that surprised her.

There had never been a question that she would show up for work. Eva had driven straight to the airport after Penny flagged them down on the road to give Grace her purse. She'd broken the speed limit by double digits to catch up to them, and when they pulled over on the shoulder she appeared at Grace's window, a sad smile on her face.

She handed her the purse and kissed her cheek. "I'm not sure what happened, but I really enjoyed meeting you."

She couldn't help but smile. Penny was incredibly sincere. "I'm glad I met you, too."

"You know, it's funny. I never would have thought Pollock was your favorite painter. That was a nice surprise."

She didn't know what to say. They were sitting on the side of the highway and Penny's random comment blindsided her. It wasn't until hours later she realized it was a supreme compliment.

"I'd like to keep in touch," she added.

She nodded and promised to ship Penny's clothes back to her.

Eva had already purchased two tickets home. That was Eva. She just knew things. *Obviously things I don't understand.* She'd left Grace alone with her thoughts for the entire flight and the drive back to her house. And there was much to think about. Her mind replayed the night in the pool house, and different images quickly journeyed through her memory—drinking the Root of Passion, kissing Lena and falling into Logan's arms after she'd climaxed.

By the time Eva pulled her Porsche into Grace's driveway, she'd resolved to forget the entire weekend, burn Margo's asinine list, and toss the oak box and its Root of Passion into the trash.

"Thanks," she said with a slight smile.

She turned to go, but Eva caught her arm. "Grace, I'm sorry things turned out like this. I just had to make sure you were safe."

"I know. I appreciate it."

Eva chuckled and stroked the fine leather of Penny's bomber jacket. "I'll admit, you look incredibly sexy, but it's just not you."

The comment stung, and while a part of her agreed, another part was offended. She gazed at Eva, who wore an amused expression. *It's all a joke to her. She thinks you look like a whore.*

"So, if this isn't me, then what is?"

"Well... you're *you*," she sputtered. "You know, Dr. Grace Owens, dependable, responsible—beautiful," she quickly added. "That's the Grace I love." Her fingers caressed Grace's cheek. "I don't know who the hell this is."

Neither do I.

Lost in her thoughts again, she didn't realize she'd maneuvered her BMW into the Thomas Road left turn lane until a horn honked behind her. She looked around, gaining her bearings. She couldn't even remember arriving at her car or driving out of the garage.

Great job, Grace.

She passed the street that led to her office without remorse. It was Monday, and since she didn't have surgery she knew she should address the mountain of paperwork that awaited her. She also had an appointment with her boss, the director of the practice, the man who signed her paycheck. None of that seemed important as she turned right onto Fifteenth Avenue.

She glanced to her left, noticing the entrance to Encanto Park, one of Phoenix's largest and oldest parks. She swerved, crossing two lanes of traffic, and pulled into the parking lot. She'd been here a few times for company picnics. One woman, in her effort to find interesting dating spots, had actually taken her canoeing. She laughed when she thought of the two of them attempting to steer the slim little boat. They ended up in a shouting match, and she had to call Margo for a ride home.

The memory reminded Grace that canoes weren't the only water transportation available, and she set out in search of the boathouse. The park was virtually empty except for some vagrants, parents with young children and a few executives eating their lunch on a bench, their ties askew or their high-heeled shoes discarded. She had crossed two bridges and found herself near the lagoon when her cell phone chimed. *Margo.*

Eva had undoubtedly called her after the previous night's disaster, and she wanted to debrief. Maybe she wanted to apologize, or maybe she wanted to chastise her for being so naïve, but Grace only wanted to be alone.

The boathouse sat at the corner of the lagoon and she grinned when she saw the paddleboats sitting next to the canoes. The boatswain was engrossed in an episode of *All my Children* and made a quick promise to settle their business when she returned.

"Just stay out for as long as you want," she said as Grace headed toward the dock.

She untied the boat closest to the water and climbed aboard. After a few revolutions it surged forward, and she was on her way. The steering mechanism, a tall lever, was hard to move, but she eventually maneuvered away from the dock. She pumped vigorously, her thighs and calves grateful for the workout. She remembered that it had been almost a week since her last morning run.

She pedaled until the novelty wore off, which happened to be in the upper half moon of the lagoon on the opposite side of the park. She drifted, listening to the water sloshing beneath her as the tiny currents beat against the metal boat.

There has to be some symbolism in this somewhere.

She focused on the green plants surrounding the lagoon and the clouds that passed overhead. If she stared at them intently, she could watch the gray and white puffs slide by. Her mind, though, slipped to the weekend, as she knew it would. There were so many contradictions—Logan's incredible tenderness juxtaposed against her deception, the Root of Passion and the Ecstasy, and the sheer exhilaration she'd felt the entire time. *The weekend of unexpected opportunities.* Now, she floated in a rickety old paddleboat in what was definitely stagnant water, when she should be a ball of kinesthetic energy surging through Monday, the hardest workday.

She decided she wouldn't return to the boathouse until she figured out her life. It was impractical to think she could dismiss the last forty-eight hours and deny they had occurred. She was changed, and her professional life could be jeopardized if she was vulnerable. She thought of Penny's theory and hoped she was right. Maybe she needed to find the balance between Dr. Grace Owens and Grace Owens, the woman—who could look really hot if she wanted to.

Okay, Grace. You're a scientist. Approach this from an analytical perspective. Examine your dependent and independent variables, employ the scientific method and draw your conclusions.

She listed her feelings, which included anger, sadness, betrayal and confusion. All were important and woven together. She was just beginning to pull apart the strands when she heard chugging behind her. She turned to see Margo paddling like a maniac.

"Unbelievable," she muttered.

"Aren't you impressed?" Margo asked as her boat drifted alongside Grace.

"How did you find me? I thought you were still in Morocco."

"When my best friend is in trouble, I'm here. I took an early flight home. Now, as to how I found you, I'll only give you clues. GPS system, friends with benefits and a great memory that recalled a conversation we once had about paddleboats."

She shook her head in amazement. "I am impressed. But you didn't have to come out here. There's nothing you can do."

"Of course there is. I can listen and I can provide sage advice. I can point out all of your faulty logic as you try to rationalize your love life and dismiss the weekend."

"What makes you think I'm going to forget the weekend?"

"Because it's uncomfortable. You went places *I've* never gone, Grace. I'll admit that more than a few women have covered me in various food toppings, but I've never had a foursome!"

"You don't have to yell," she said, her cheeks coloring.

Margo looked around. "Who would hear us? Now, where are you with Logan?"

"I hope I never see her again, not after what she did."

"So, you're not interested in her."

"No, and I don't think she was ever interested in me, really. I was just another conquest."

"Okay, what about Eva?"

She paused. Eva still had feelings for her, and the fact that she'd come all the way to Vegas to get her was impressive. Yet, she represented the past and clearly had her pigeonholed as a boring prude. "I'm not sure. Undecided. Doubtful."

Margo nodded. "Fair enough. How about Dina? Could she be a possibility?"

She shrugged and fiddled with the steering wheel. "I hardly know her."

"Ah, but she knows you. And she's interested."

She raised an eyebrow. She recalled the night when she'd flashed her. "That's interesting."

Margo clapped her hands and giggled. "Excellent. Now then, what about you? Do you feel changed?"

"Yes, but I'm thinking it was all a sham. It was the Ecstasy. I was just responding to external stimuli."

"Don't go all medical on me, sweetie. I'm just an average citizen. Look, the Ecstasy may have triggered some of your responses, but it couldn't account for everything. She only drugged you twice, right?"

She nodded. "That's what she said, and I believe her."

"Okay, if that's true, then why did you to go to bed with Michelle? What made you decide to go to Vegas? Why did you sleep with Logan?"

She didn't have any answers. She'd like to think she'd finally unleashed her wild desires, but the actuality of her thrusting open her milquetoast cage and roaring out of it was unfathomable. It was more likely that a mysterious, unexplainable potion had taken control of her body.

"Do you really think it was the Root of Passion?"

Margo shrugged and threw up her hands. "Honestly, I have no idea." She looked toward the shore. "When I bought it, I knew it was unusual. There was something special about it. Maybe *I* was drugged." She looked back at her. "Does it matter?"

"Of course it does. I've just spent the last forty-eight hours engaging in the most unbelievable behavior of my life, and I need an explanation."

Margo laughed. "You're such a scientist. Why does there always have to be an answer? Why do you always have to know?"

"Because I do. That's who I am."

"Well, this time you may have to rely on a little faith."

Faith. There was a word she rarely thought about. As a child, she'd heard it endlessly during church but as she grew older and turned to her studies, church didn't seem to fit. In her mind, faith was anathema to science.

She reached into her purse and withdrew the oak box. She'd dropped it into the trash can three times—and retrieved it. She couldn't bring herself to part with it. But it was either responsible for her unsafe behavior, or it was a symbol of faith in the unproven—an idea her mind couldn't process. She drew back her arm and stared out into the murky lagoon water. This would at least be a permanent goodbye.

"What are you doing?" Margo asked.

"I'm getting rid of this. I'm not sure what it is, but I'm done with it. I'm not drinking another drop."

"Wait!"

She jerked to the right and saw Margo's hand extended toward her. "Please give me that. If you have no further use for it, that's fine. But I paid a lot of money for it and I'd like to know what that potion's made of. I'll bet you would, too."

The idea of using the remaining Root of Passion to answer scientific questions appealed to her. She tossed her the box. Margo dropped it into her purse and started pedaling.

"Okay, let's get out of here. I want you to promise me something."

"What."

"The next time you have a personal crisis, can we please pick a less remote and odorous location to meet, one that doesn't require me to exercise?"

Her talk with Margo proved to be enough therapy, and while she still didn't have all the answers about her life, she returned to her office and completed all of the paperwork that awaited her. By the time she pulled onto her street it was nearly dark, but there was no mistaking Pepper, the Great Dane, trotting down her driveway with Dina close at his side.

"Hey," she called as Grace stepped out of the car.

She couldn't help but smile. The woman always seemed to be so cheerful. "Hi. How are you?"

She scratched Pepper behind his ears and he wiggled his big head at her. He wasn't on a leash, but unlike their previous meeting he stayed next to his master.

"I'm great. Your friend asked me to collect your papers and mail. I left it on your dining room table for you."

"Thanks."

"No problem. How was your trip?"

She paused, unsure of how to answer the question. *Unbelievable? Inconceivable?* "It was fine. Just a chance to relax."

Dina raised an eyebrow and laughed. "In Vegas? I guess it depends on who you went with and what you did."

She blushed. "I'll just take the Fifth."

They both laughed, and when neither could think of anything else to say, their gazes fell to Pepper. He burped loudly and the awkwardness disappeared.

"I'm sorry. He had a big dinner," Dina said.

"I imagine every meal would be big for him."

Dina chuckled and shuffled her feet. "Yeah. So, I was wondering if you might want to go hear some jazz this Saturday."

She smiled, pleased. "I'd like that."

"Great," Dina said. She took a step toward her, and Grace could see her beautiful blue-green eyes under the streetlamp's glow. "Any chance you might wear that incredibly sexy dress? You know, the one that has trouble covering your body?"

She laughed nervously. "I might. But don't you think I'll be terribly overdressed for a jazz club?" *You're flirting, Grace. You never flirt, at least, not very well.*

They stared at each other, both grinning, and she was certain they were both remembering the night she flashed Dina.

Dina shook her head slowly. "No. I think that dress would be absolutely perfect for what I have planned."

Chapter Twenty

When Grace finally exited the OR after a grueling three-hour surgery to repair a damaged aorta, Eva was leaning against the wall, obviously waiting for her. Grace sighed and offered a slight smile, hoping her clear fatigue would send a message. When Eva followed her down the hallway, she knew it had not.

"I think we need to talk."

"Not now. I'm exhausted."

"I've called you half a dozen times since Sunday and you haven't returned my calls."

That was true. She didn't really have anything to say that she hadn't already said. She was grateful that Eva had come to Vegas and revealed Logan for the liar she was, but she'd said her thank-yous, and that was all there was to it.

"Grace, please." She grabbed her arm, forcing her to stop.

"What?" She knew she sounded annoyed, but Eva of all people should know that she never mixed her personal and professional life.

"Look, are you okay?" Eva whispered, conscious of the fact that they were standing in a public corridor. "I mean, you didn't have any side effects from the E, did you?"

"No," she said gently. It was kind of Eva to think of her health first. "I'm fine. I just need to sort out my life, you know. A lot happened over the weekend."

"Hopefully you can't remember most of it."

"Actually it's all rather clear, and if I'm honest with myself it was the most fun I've had in years." As she said the words, Eva frowned, and she realized she'd hurt her without meaning to. "I'm sorry," she quickly said, "that didn't come out well."

Eva crossed her arms and shrugged. "It's your life. But I'll admit, I was unbelievably shocked when I saw you get off that motorcycle. It was entirely surreal. Grace Owens riding a motorcycle and looking like a second-rate tramp."

She held her tongue and took a deep breath. Yes, she imagined after the drinking game and the long ride her appearance was unsightly, but she still looked sexy and Eva had cajoled her many times about her wardrobe which she affectionately called the bland and blasé.

She chose her words carefully as two doctors exited the OR and passed by with cordial nods. "I can't talk about this now. Please understand. I'll call you."

"I'd like to see you again," Eva blurted. "I think we should give it another try."

She wasn't surprised after what Margo had said, but her timing was horrible. She couldn't put into words how she was feeling. It was complicated, and every nerve in her body was spent, the operation draining her physically and mentally. She had no emotional energy left to share.

She started to walk away without responding, and Eva muttered, "You'll never change."

The comment stung, because she'd come to realize how poorly she'd behaved during her relationship with Eva, but anger instantly smothered her guilt and she whirled around to face her.

"Stop it. I'm grateful that you came to Vegas, and you were right about Logan, and you're probably right to be angry about the past. I didn't treat you very well. I'm sorry. I apologize. You're a better person than me. Is that what you want to hear?"

Her eyes grew wide, and her jaw dropped. "I don't think I'm better than you," she finally said. "I just want us to be together. Would you ever consider it?"

She closed her eyes for a moment, fatigue overtaking her. "I'll think about it. If you want an answer now, then it's no."

When their eyes met, Eva's were clouded with doubt. "Sure, I'll wait," she said.

She watched Eva walk away, and she suddenly realized she had no desire to rekindle their fire. It would be too much work, and it might not lead anywhere. They would have to dismantle the past, like taking apart a broken machine and then rebuilding it with the hopes that it would be better than the first model. And she didn't think the old Eva would tolerate the new Grace for very long. *She says you'll never change because she doesn't want you to change, not really.*

She remembered Eva's shock at the sight of her, covered in beer, wearing the sexy biker outfit. Before the plane took off, Eva had shuttled her into an airport shop, where she bought a new tank top to wear onto the plane. Still, clad in the leather jacket, many of the male passengers stared unabashedly, until their female companions poked them in the ribs and snarled at her. A flight attendant took a particular interest in her, offering her pillows and blankets, and flashing a killer smile more than once in her direction.

She giggled at the memory and halted her trek to the doctor's lounge. *That's significant, Gracie. You liked the attention and you felt sexy. You flaunted your sexuality.* She leaned against the closest wall and sighed. There really was only one question she couldn't answer. Had she uncovered the key to her happiness, or was the new Grace just a chemical reaction to drugs and the Root of Passion?

Chapter Twenty-one

No city thrilled Margo like New York. Whenever she landed at JFK she extended her layover by a day or two, enjoying a mini-vacation a couple times a month. Even after several years of these pilgrimages she never tired of the noise and the often surly New Yorkers, and since the city was ever-changing, there was always something to do. She frequented the off-Broadway plays, visited the traveling exhibits at the Met and usually detoured to Fifth Avenue for shopping.

She always came alone, never inviting her colleagues or friends to join her. She was comforted by her solitude, enjoying the new experiences without the obligation to share with a traveling companion. Most people couldn't bear to see New York without someone else, but she couldn't imagine it any other way. The little jaunts to New York were an injection, ones that she always anticipated.

As the train whirred through the stations, taking her closer to Greenwich Village, she smiled slightly, remembering her first visits when she'd study her map of the subway system, before she knew the stops by heart. It was all second nature to her now and she no longer looked like a tourist. She belonged.

The village was one of her favorite places, home to diversity and eclecticism. She could spend hours sitting at a café and people watching, amazed by their indifference to normalcy and their willingness to wear their self-esteem like a suit of armor. By the time she'd finished an espresso, she'd undoubtedly see hair colored any shade of the rainbow, transvestites on their way to work and behavior that, in any other U.S. city, would bring the cops. Once she'd seen two men, apparently in the heat of new love, go at it so hard against a streetlamp that she turned away in embarrassment.

The train stopped and more passengers flowed in and out of the cars. Three stops later she arrived at Fourteenth Street. As she climbed the steps, leaving the subterranean world and its interesting smells, the sunlight kissed her face and temporarily blinded her. She shielded her eyes and looked straight ahead at her destination, the Greenwich.

The old twelve-story building loomed over the corner of West Thirteenth Street and Sixth. She'd learned it was originally built in 1904, and converted to condominiums around the new millennium. From the outside it still resembled an office building with rows of parallel square windows cutting into the gray mortar. But she knew that the lofts inside commanded seven figures and the Greenwich was a premier real estate site, primarily because of its outstanding location at the heart of the village.

When Vonnie, the doorman, saw her approaching, he grinned broadly. "Ms. Margo, it's a pleasure to see you again. You're back rather quickly," he added, remembering that her last visit was only six weeks prior.

"The timing was right. How is she?"

Vonnie's smile crumpled, and he shook his head. She could

always count on him to be honest and keep her informed. He'd even taken her cell number, promising to call her immediately if something terrible happened.

"She's had a bad few weeks. Family's been up twice, and she's been to a string of doctors. I don't know what it means, and you know how Rose is."

She nodded. She did indeed. Rose never shared anything about her illness, unwilling to burden others with her pain and grief. "Damn thing's already taking too much of my time," she'd told Margo. "I'm not handing over an extra *second*."

"Thanks, Vonnie," she said, crossing the lobby.

Yet, instead of heading immediately to the elevator, she slowed her footsteps as she realized she needed more time to collect her thoughts. She ducked into the powder room and dropped onto a chaise lounge, relieved that she was alone. She fumbled through her purse until she found the oak box and held the vial in her hand. She caressed the smooth glass, convincing herself that she was doing the right thing, that giving Rose the second vial wouldn't make her sicker, or worse, kill her.

Rose Smith was as unassuming as her name. Margo had met her three years before on a flight from L.A. to New York. Originally, Margo was assigned to the coach seating, but at the last minute, Norma decided that Margo would oversee first class, and Rose was one of the nine call buzzers that she answered to for five hours.

She was accustomed to first class passengers who could be far more demanding than the common folk forced to sit in coach. It was not unusual for her to answer twenty different calls from one person in first class. She quickly learned why Norma had wanted to switch. A codependent, frequent-flying CEO and a recently discovered starlet drunk with her power over the service industry kept her moving for the first three hours.

When she finally had a moment to stop and catch her breath, she noticed a rather attractive dark-haired woman in her late twenties, reading a travel guide on Greece. Her doe eyes raced across the page, and she moved her lush lips just slightly as she read the words. She'd later learn her name was Rose.

She'd paid no attention to her during the first round of drinks, barely looking up from her notepad, her mind focused on appeasing the CEO who was legendary for his complaints to the airline. Rose sat unobtrusively in the last row nursing the same scotch Margo had originally served her.

"Excuse me, but I just wanted to make sure you were comfortable."

She nodded politely, blinking her soft brown eyes. "I'm fine. Thank you for asking."

If everyone could be as polite as you, she thought. Only then did she notice the walker leaning against the adjoining seat and the airline blanket that covered her legs. She hadn't greeted the passengers in first class and hadn't seen Rose board the aircraft. How well could she walk? The idea of someone so kind and polite being disabled tore at her heart.

"If you need any assistance, you know, with anything, please don't hesitate to ask."

Rose must have heard the discomfort in her voice and smiled. "I'm fine, really. And despite my penchant for scotch, I've developed an iron bladder over the years. It's just too hard to maneuver in and out of those postage stamp-sized lavatories."

She laughed and instantly felt it was inappropriate. Would Rose think she was mocking her disability?

"I'm so sorry. I shouldn't laugh."

"Why not?" Rose asked indignantly. "That was a joke. It was a *funny* joke with a central metaphor. I would be upset if you didn't laugh."

"Then, I'm glad I did."

Although Rose didn't press the call button for the remainder of the flight, Margo periodically glanced in her direction, fascinated by her humor and wit. Each time the picture was the same—Rose's face buried in the travel book, clearly fascinated by what she was learning.

When the plane landed, she assumed her station at the front, greeting each passenger as he or she exited. She noticed

Rose waited until everyone on the plane, including the coach passengers, had debarked. Only then did she move the walker into the aisle, pull herself up against the headrest in front of her seat and slip on her backpack.

She automatically went to her side, but Rose was shaking her head.

"Don't you dare offer to help me. I'm perfectly capable of exiting a plane, except perhaps in the event of an emergency landing. In that case, you may save my sorry ass."

Again she laughed as Rose stepped into the walker and slowly pattered down the aisle. *She's right. She's obviously done this before, although she walks like a ninety-year-old woman.* She remained at the back of first class, watching her progress, trying to stay out of the way.

When she reached the very front, she turned slightly and said, "So, have you been to a lot of places?"

"Yes, I've been to every city where we fly."

"Do they ever let you off this toothpaste tube or do you have to sleep in the jump seat?"

She stifled a chuckle. "No, we have a layover. Actually, I'm here for a few more days to see the sites. I love New York."

Rose smiled, and although she was still several feet away, she thought she saw tears welling in her eyes.

"I love it, too. I'd never leave if I didn't have to, but…"

Her voice trailed off in sadness, and Margo sensed her trip to L.A. hadn't been pleasurable. She assumed it had something to do with the walker, for what else could a bright, attractive young woman have to be sad about?

"Listen, I'm getting some food from Zabar's and pigging out at my condo. I'll bet it beats whatever you can afford on the lousy per diem they're paying you. Wanna come?"

She'd readily agreed, curious to learn about Rose Smith. They had spent most of the night eating scrumptious meat and cheeses and drinking a French wine that she could never afford. Rose had insisted on opening with a synopsis of her life story.

"If I don't explain my injury and my wealth, you won't hear

another thing I say. And I really don't want to talk about my biography. I want to know what it's like to travel the world, and I want you to describe the Eiffel Tower and the Taj Mahal. Fair enough?"

It had been more than fair. Margo learned Rose's family was incredibly wealthy but all the money couldn't stop the illness that was ravaging her body. She'd been disabled in a terrible car accident and suffered from several complications that brought on a multitude of complications that she couldn't pronounce and didn't care about.

She often traveled to L.A. to visit a specialist, but her life was primarily confined to the walls of her expensive loft, which at least afforded her an extraordinary view of New York.

Trips to the Greenwich became a habit for Margo whenever she visited New York. She brought pictures of where she'd visited and recounted the unique beauty of the wonderful cities around the world. Rose would listen with her eyes closed, and, once she'd created the entire picture in her head, her eyes would fly open and she'd rifle another ten questions. It was an exhausting exercise, but one Margo was glad to endure for her new friend.

They were so much alike, a stark difference from Grace and herself. And while Grace would always hold the position of best friend in her life, there was a connection with Rose that she could never duplicate. And for the longest time she ignored that connection, refusing to acknowledge that she'd fallen in love with a sickly woman nearly twenty years her junior.

When she finally told her how she felt, Rose simply nodded. "Of course, I knew that. You mean you're just figuring it out?"

She was stunned. "You knew I loved you? Do you love me?"

Rose stirred her tea and stared at the table. "Margo, I'm only going to say this once, so I need you to listen very carefully. God is indeed cruel. If he wasn't, he never would have placed us on that plane together that day, given my medical history and our natural chemistry." She looked up and took a deep breath before she continued. "Unlike you, I've thought about this for months—years. I've spent hours planning this speech, for the time when you finally saw the truth. I know you're just realizing all of this now, so it's not even fair, but I've already decided for both of us."

"What does that mean?" she interjected.

"It means that while I love you, and I believe you love me, our love has… limitations. You know I can never be sexual with you, and I know you are extremely physical. It's a need for you. I want you to promise me that you will continue to take lovers and that you will tell no one of our feelings for each other, not even Grace."

She'd been stunned. "Why not?"

"Our love is doomed," Rose whispered. "You know that. And I will not be subjected to well-intentioned dinners with your friends or the pitying looks of your family when you take your girlfriend home to meet them. I just can't do it." She paused and stared into her eyes. "You must continue as though there is nothing between us. Lead your wanton life and regale me with your escapades. It's how I'll finish my life and know that you'll continue with yours when I'm gone."

Rose's speech had moved her. It was so eloquent and honest. She'd simply nodded and abided by her wishes. They'd never spoken of it again.

Over the last six months, though, when she called, Rose was either in L.A., or she wasn't feeling well enough for a visit. She could no longer walk, restricted to a wheelchair, and Margo imagined her time with Rose was finite, and any visit could be the last. She wanted to give her something amazing, but she didn't want to violate the agreements they'd made. The Root of Passion was so unexpected and outside the realm of possibility that she hoped Rose might see the value.

A knock on the door erased her thoughts. Vonnie stuck his head around the corner. "Margo, are you okay? You've been in here a long time and I just wanted to check on you. Is there anything I can get you? Should I call Miss Rose?"

"No, no," she said quickly. "I was just putting on my face. I'm ready now."

She jumped up and allowed him to hold the door for her as she went to the elevators. *How will you explain this to Rose?*

She planned her speech on the ride up to the twelfth floor, a passionate plea full of wit and emotion. If she'd learned anything over the last few years, it was the gentle persuasion tactics that appealed to Rose and gave Margo what she wanted—namely, a physical connection with Rose. After they'd declared their love, it took three months before Rose agreed to kiss her, and another two months before she believed that Margo desired her, wanted to give her as much sexual gratification as possible, at least from the waist up. And, as she suspected, Rose's greatest joy came from pleasuring her and listening to her moans of ecstasy.

The Rose who greeted her at the door was almost a stranger. She'd lost more weight and her cheeks were hollow. Although she'd always looked older than her twenty-eight years, the skin hung so loosely on her body that Margo wouldn't have been able to guess her age if they'd been strangers.

She hid her shock immediately and leaned over the wheelchair for a kiss. "Darling, I've missed you."

Their lips touched and she felt her knees go weak. Rose's lips were always luscious, and when she closed her eyes she imagined a different Rose, a strong, beautiful Rose that matched those lips.

"I'm not up for much," Rose said wearily. "I sent my newest aide to the store so we could be alone for awhile."

Margo wheeled her into the living room and busied herself preparing their tea. It was a ritual that dated back to their first meeting, one that never changed.

"What happened to the woman who was here when I visited before?"

Rose shook her head. "I couldn't stand her. She spent every moment on her iPod and chomping on gum. She was totally worthless."

She said nothing, but she was surprised at Rose's judgment. It was unusual for her to be so caustic. "Is this one any better?"

"Quite. She's an older lady who's had much experience with

the nearly dead." Margo shot her a glance and she shrugged. "I'm sorry, darling, but it's a fact."

She brought the tea and faced her. If she didn't recite her speech soon, she'd lose her nerve. "I've accepted the fact that I can't control the future and what's inevitable, but I think I've found a way to control the moment and give you—us—a gift."

"What are you talking about?"

She dug through her purse and held out the box. "I have a present for you."

Rose opened it and her expression grew quizzical as she examined the vial and the lavender liquid. "What's this?"

"It's called the Root of Passion. A few swallows and you're sexual energy is free. I never would have believed it could work, but I've been conducting my own clinical study on a few other people and I'm a believer."

Rose laughed heartily. "Oh, Margo, dear, have you totally lost it? You're telling me that you believe in magic potions?"

"Watch," she said, as she shook the vial. On cue, the lavender separated into its red and blue bases.

"My God, honey, where in hell did you get this? Is this some kind of sick joke?"

She took her hand and squeezed it. "It's not. I can't explain it. I bought it in Rio and I've seen its effects. It can help us, honey."

Skepticism was all over her face. "Help us do what?"

She stared into her eyes. "I want you to have an orgasm. I want us to make love, and I want you to be completely and totally satisfied."

Her shoulders sank and she seemed to shrink into the wheelchair. "Why, Margo? Why are you doing this? Isn't it enough? I thought what we had was enough for you."

"It is enough for me, honey, but this is about *you*. It's what I want to give you."

Rose set her tea down and wheeled out of the room. She knew she'd upset her, but she didn't understand why. She found her in her bedroom, facing the door, crying.

"Honey, what's wrong?"

161

"I know you say this is for me, but it's really for you. It'll mean that you can finally get the sick girl off. The one that got away, the one who never cried out, 'Margo!' during the throes of passion. It will mean that you have done the impossible—"

"Stop! How dare you treat me this way? I'd do anything for you. I *have* done everything you've asked. I've denied our love to everyone who matters to me. I've allowed all of my co-workers to think I'm nothing but a shallow slut, incapable of finding lasting love. I've listened to my friends talk about the amazing people in their lives, unable to tell them that I've actually met someone who's *better* than anyone they could ever know."

She knelt in front of Rose, holding up the vial. It hadn't been the speech she'd planned, but from the surprised look on Rose's face, she'd made her point. Rose took the vial and stared into her eyes.

"I'd never hurt you," Margo whispered.

Rose flipped off the cork and threw back her head. Margo watched the Root of Passion trail out the vial and slide between her incredible lips. When the contents were gone, she leaned forward and her body shook spastically.

"Rose! What's wrong?" Margo held her arms while her head flailed from side to side. "Oh, my God!"

Suddenly, Rose's body froze, and she grinned. "Just kidding."

"I'm going to kill you myself," she said slowly. "That was an awful trick," she added, pulling away from Rose. She was incredibly angry—at Rose and herself. *What if the potion harmed her?* It was too late to undo what she'd done.

She sat on Rose's bed and buried her face in her hands. Rose was right. She was selfish, rationalizing that if they had sex, Rose would be so grateful and enlightened.

"Margo?"

Unable to look at her, she headed for the door. "I'm going to go. I'm sorry. I'll call you next week."

"Margo, wait. Please don't leave. We don't have time for dramatic exits. There may not be another visit, and truthfully, what if I'm not around to get your call next week?" She chuckled and said, "Then you'd feel *really* shitty."

Margo smiled slightly and gazed into the soft brown eyes she loved. "I would. I'd hate myself for wasting our precious time."

"And it is precious." Rose glanced at her wristwatch and frowned. "Now we only have another forty-five minutes or so before my babysitter returns. I sent her to eight different stores, but she's terribly efficient and can't take a hint. We need to be naked and under these covers *now*."

In less than a minute, Margo had shed her clothes and helped Rose into bed. Their lips immediately erased the six weeks of absence, and Rose cupped her breasts.

"I'm sorry your little potion didn't work, darling, but you'll be happy to know I still find you terribly attractive."

"Thank God," Margo gasped, as Rose's teeth pulled gently on her nipple.

She let Rose take the lead, repositioning herself occasionally to give her full access to her body.

"Is it a little warm in here?" Rose asked as Margo hovered over her, her center glistening in desire.

"I know where it's a little warm," Margo said.

Rose nestled her tongue against the folds of her labia, exploring, caressing and sucking just enough to keep her at the brink of climax.

"Now, honey, please," she whimpered.

"I'm not ready to let you go yet," Rose stated plainly.

"I don't think I can wait."

Rose licked her clitoris and slid her finger deep inside. They found a rhythm, and Margo fought against the orgasm suffocating her body, wanting to savor the incredible feeling for as long as possible.

"Keep going," she groaned. "Don't stop."

"You'll come when I tell you to come," Rose hissed. "And I want you to come now."

She pressed her hand against Margo's pelvis, and it threw her over the edge into a chasm of pleasure. When she stopped trembling, she fell into Rose's arms and kissed her gently.

"I love your power over me. You make me feel so good."

To return the favor, she climbed on top of Rose, trailing kisses down her neck and over her breasts. Out of sheer habit, she spread her legs and massaged her thighs. Although Rose had no sensation below her waist, it was a standard move in Margo's repertoire of lovemaking, and Rose certainly didn't mind. In fact, what Margo didn't share was that Rose was frequently wet between her legs, her body responding to the sex despite the lack of nerve endings that would have allowed her to enjoy it.

"More," Rose said. "I want more."

She was surprised. Rose rarely said anything while she pleasured her. Most of the time she assumed Rose was humoring her and feigning enjoyment.

"What else do you want me to do, baby?"

Her face contorted into a painful expression, and she grabbed her head. "I don't know. Something. Anything. Figure it out!"

She froze. Never had Rose been this way. She immediately brought her lips to Rose's and massaged her arms.

"Against me. Press yourself against me," Rose said, in a commanding voice. "I want your clit against mine."

She obliged, allowing her full weight to rest against Rose's frail little body. The act aroused her again, and she blanched at the idea of having a second orgasm when Rose couldn't have one.

Quick little gasps escaped Rose's lips, and her eyes seemed to focus on something far away. She wasn't looking at Margo. "Harder," she said. "Harder, darling!"

Margo slowly ground her hips in a circle, and just as she was about to roll off Rose, convinced she was hurting her, a tiny cry broke through her lips, and then she was sobbing.

"What have I done? Darling, are you all right?"

Rose didn't answer, but her sobs turned into wails.

Margo jumped off the bed, not knowing what to do. She reached for the phone and was about to press nine-one-one when Rose waved her back to the bed.

164

"No, darling. Don't. I'm not hurt."

She took Margo's hands and kissed them, rubbing them against her wet cheeks. When she looked up, she was laughing. Margo's expression must have been total shock, for she leaned over and kissed her.

"I'm sorry that I scared you. I really need to thank you and your little potion. Sweetheart, I just had an orgasm!"

Chapter Twenty-two

Grace twirled once in front of her closet mirror, the silky black folds of the cocktail dress rippling with the motion. She stared at her reflection, critically assessing her appearance. Something was definitely different but she couldn't explain it. She started at the top of her head and studied herself—all the way to the polish on her toenails. Her hairstyle was the same. The shoes weren't new. She'd applied her makeup the same way, but she realized she'd started wearing thicker eyeliner to accentuate her eyes. Maybe that was it.

Maybe you're just out of practice.

She hadn't gone out in nearly a year, and while she never would have chosen the slinky dress for a first date, Dina had requested it and she was thrilled to comply.

The doorbell rang and she glanced at the clock in the dining room. Dina was fifteen minutes early. She had a witty comment prepared as she flung open the door, but it died on her lips when she saw Logan standing on the porch. She wore her standard cargo shorts and blue denim work shirt and she was carrying a small package wrapped in brown mailing paper. When she smiled, Grace's heart melted again. *I didn't need the Root of Passion for that to happen.*

"Hello, Grace. I'm sorry I missed you at the hospital. I needed to see you so I hope you don't mind. I had a friend look up your address."

Grace raised an eyebrow. "That friend wouldn't be your drug connection by any chance, would it?"

Logan ignored the question and said, "I'll make sure all of your clothes are shipped here."

She nodded, remembering the stunning green dress. *What would Dina say if she saw me in that?*

Desperate to change the subject, she asked, "How's your father?" Chester had been home from the hospital for a week.

"He's great, thanks to you. He's so happy to be home."

"I'm sure. I thought you'd gone on to another assignment."

"No, I was just avoiding you. I didn't think you wanted to see me and I didn't want his doctor to be uncomfortable in front of him."

"How considerate. You're right. I don't want to see you."

She started to close the door but Logan stepped in its path. "Please, Grace. I just need a few minutes."

"You have nothing to say that I want to hear. Now, if you'll please get out of my doorway, I'm getting ready for a date."

Logan remained planted in the doorframe, and she grinned broadly. "I was hoping that was the reason you looked so hot. I guess you're working on number five."

She glanced up, surprised by Logan's forwardness.

Logan leaned closer and whispered, "Frankly, I prefer the biker outfit."

Maybe it was her charm, or maybe it was what she wanted to hear. She didn't have time for analysis so she opened the door and motioned her inside.

"I won't stay long. I just wanted to say that I'm sorry our weekend ended the way it did, and I wanted to give you this."

She held out the package and Grace tore off the paper, exposing a red leather photo album. The words *Our Trip* were stamped in gold across the front. The first black-and-white photo was of Grace listening to Chester's heart, her expression serious. Next, she was sitting in the cocktail lounge at the airport, her posture so ramrod straight she could see the veins in her neck. She was wringing her hands and her lips were a straight line of tension. She remembered a few times when Logan had aimed the large lens in her direction, but some of the pictures were a surprise. She looked awkward and timid coming out of the clothing shop wearing the amazing green dress, but her breath caught at the next shot—asleep on the hotel bed, naked, the sheets haphazardly tossed to the side. Logan must have stood on a chair, for the camera hovered above Grace, exposing her from head to toe, lying on her stomach, her blond hair caressing the side of her face. She thought the photo was incredibly artistic and erotic.

She blushed and turned the page to two pictures she remembered, one of her between Kazmar and Lena and the other standing next to Penny, who looked radiant in her red cocktail dress. While Grace stared into the camera, Penny stared at her, smiling, almost beaming. It was one of those pictures where one subject was prepared for the click of the shutter and the other was caught a moment too soon, revealing her private thoughts. She gazed at the expression on Penny's face. She didn't know what to think.

She laughed when she turned the page, for staring back at her was a woman she didn't really know. One photo showed her astride the Harley, leaning against the backrest, her fingers laced behind her head. The tiny T-shirt had ridden up, revealing much of her belly, and her eyes were closed. It was the most sexual picture she ever had taken.

The last photo was a headshot of her on stage, her hair a

mess, singing into the microphone a'la Janis Joplin. She thought she remembered that moment. It was near the end of the second verse when she'd decided to throw herself into the song with total abandon, pushing Dr. Grace Owens entirely out of her psyche. *That's how you look on E, Grace.* She returned to the photo of the woman sitting in the airport cocktail lounge and couldn't believe the difference. *I certainly don't feel like the same person.*

"May I?"

Logan took the book from her and flipped to the picture of her in the bed. "I'd like to use that one in my next show, if you don't mind."

"What?" Grace asked, suddenly thinking of thousands of people ogling her body. "Why would you ever want to do that?"

Logan wrapped her arms around Grace. "When I look at this picture, I see the Sistine Chapel, St. Paul's Cathedral, and so many of the other wonderful places I've traveled. This is a beautiful photo, Grace. It's the epitome of how I will remember you."

God, she's so smooth.

Their lips connected, and as suddenly as it had begun, it stopped. Logan stepped away and leaned against the dining room wall.

"I think it's better if I stay over here," she said. "I don't think your date would approve if she found us in bed together."

Grace steadied herself against one of the chairs. "How do you do this to me? I should be furious with you. You drugged me."

"I know," Logan said quietly. "I'm sorry about that. The truth is, I started to fall for you, and I needed an insurance policy."

"What do you mean?"

"Something to keep us apart. I meant what I told you, Grace. Relationships don't work for me, not with this job. And I'm not a moronic bitch who keeps trying to be involved when she already knows the outcome. It wouldn't be fair."

"I agree."

"But, I can't help my feelings. And I had serious feelings for you. The E served two purposes. I was truly worried that you wouldn't follow through with some of the things you really needed to do, and I knew that if you found out you'd hate me. Broken trust is the best way to prevent a relationship."

Grace shook her head. "I can't even relate to where you're coming from. But you had no right to drug me, particularly for your selfish reasons. That makes you a bitch in my book."

Logan's eyes fell to the floor. "I suppose you're right."

"What if Eva hadn't shown up? I might've never known about the E."

Logan glanced up and said quietly, "No, then I would've told you when we got back. Eva spared me the hard part, but your anger and loss of trust were inevitable."

Her lip quivered, and she willed herself not to cry. "I see."

"But if I had to do it over, I'd do the same thing. And I'm sorry if that makes you angry. It's just that when I saw you with my dad, I was so impressed. And when I started snapping the pictures in the hospital, the lens showed me another side of you, the unexplored possibilities."

She rolled her eyes. "Oh, please."

Logan reached for the photo and pointed at the picture of her in bed. "I know it sounds crazy, but I saw this photo in my head two days before I took it. I knew you would look this beautiful when you slept. The rest of these pictures were just fun. And that's what last weekend was, Grace. It was *fun*."

She couldn't disagree. The photos were the proof. What she'd said to Eva was true. She'd never had that much fun in her life. She glanced up at Logan and nodded.

"Well, I need to go." She opened the door and looked back at her. "I hope you have fun again, Grace. You can't live carefree every day, making love with strangers or playing drinking games—"

"Why not? You do," she said with a chuckle.

Logan laughed and shrugged. "Most people aren't me. You'd never want my life anyway, but I'm glad I could be a part of yours. There's someone out there for you. She's closer than you think. And thanks for saving my dad."

She left and Grace repressed an urge to cry, knowing that Dina would arrive in minutes. She took deep breaths and blinked several times to push back the tears. She ran back to the bathroom and had just finished applying her lipstick when the doorbell rang again.

"Hey," Dina said when she opened the door, a lazy smile on her face. Her eyes wandered up and down Grace's body. "You look amazing."

"You too," she said, studying Dina's skintight jeans and black dress shirt. "Just let me get my purse and I'll be ready to go."

She disappeared into the bedroom, and when she returned, Dina was holding the photo album, staring at the photo of naked Grace. She looked up from the book, her eyes smoldering.

"That must have been some trip."

"It was."

She couldn't think of anything else to say, so she stood there while Dina slowly turned each page, judging her, deciding if she wanted to date someone so free and loose. She stared at the karaoke photo for a long time, and then she finally closed the book and returned it to the table. Grace prepared herself for a quick goodbye, an evening alone and a future of hard stares every time Dina drove by.

"So, who are you?" Dina asked with a searing gaze.

The question surprised her. "I'm not sure anymore. The only way that album could have existed a month ago was with Photoshop. Now, I'm just confused."

Dina slid into her arms and stroked her back. "Then let me help you. I'm very enlightened."

"You want to make me your project?"

"I guess that's one way to put it."

Her heart beat faster. Dina's fingers traced the muscles in her back, touching each curve, exciting her.

"But you're so young," she said, her voice cracking as Dina buried her lips in the hollow of her neck. "What could you possibly teach me?"

"I'm an old soul."

Dina pressed her against the wall and deftly unclasped the ribbons of silk that covered her breasts and yanked down the zipper. The dress slid to the floor, and she closed her eyes, preparing for her body to be showered with kisses and caresses. *You want it, Gracie. You know it.*

Instead, when she opened her eyes, Dina was standing on the other side of the room, her arms crossed.

"What are you doing? I thought—"

"*You* have to want it, Grace. It's not about people doing things to you, seducing you, leading you into romance. You need to take charge."

She laughed. "Is this some sort of sex-esteem workshop?"

Dina strolled into the living room, dropped into an overstuffed chair and propped her boots onto the ottoman. Grace couldn't tell if she'd closed her eyes, ready to take a nap, or if she was studying the ceiling.

It's up to you. Do you want her? Either pull the dress back on or make a move.

She glanced at the little album on the table, and the black-and-white photos shuffled through her mind like a slideshow. She kicked off her pumps and stepped out of the dress. A patch of moonlight shone onto the living room rug like a spotlight, and for a moment she was reminded of the karaoke stage. She stood in its center, invigorated by the glow against her body, facing Dina, who stared at her intently. Even when she dropped her silk panties to the floor, Dina's gaze never wavered. She smiled slightly, and it was all Grace needed. She crawled into Dina's arms—and took charge.

Chapter Twenty-three

"I think you should take me to South America," Grace said.

Margo and Joseph simultaneously looked up from their dinners and stared at her. The request surprised Margo, since Grace and Dina had been seeing each other for two months.

"Why would you want me to do that? I think you and Dina have incredible chemistry."

"We do," Grace agreed, reaching for the bottle of merlot and pouring another glass for herself. "But she's so much younger, and I'm worried that I won't excite her for very long."

"You're not old," Joseph said. "It's not like you've got a shelf life that's about to expire. Has she complained?"

"No, I just don't think it can last. She has *so much* energy. She'd go out every night if she could. I'm much more of a homebody."

"You seem to be enjoying the night life just fine," Margo

observed. "How many times have I called you in the last month and the two of you already had plans? You were going to a club opening or a party. Your calendar is packed!"

Grace rolled her eyes. "That's all Dina. She's the social planner. She tells me what to wear and when to be ready. Half the time I don't even enjoy where we go. I'd be much more content staying home and watching a DVD, at least some of the time—"

"Is that before or after the hot sex?" Joseph asked.

Margo laughed and noticed Grace was blushing. Since the trip to Vegas, the Root of Passion and Dina, Grace was a different person. She'd learned to balance the demands of her job with a healthy social life, and, until tonight, she'd never mentioned needing any chemical help. In fact, a few of her antics worried Margo since Grace was pushing the envelope of risk-taking. She'd skydived, signed a short-term lease on a motorcycle and sent most of her wardrobe to the Salvation Army. Margo approved of *that* decision, since she was the one who'd led Grace on a three-day shopping spree through Scottsdale Fashion Square, spending thousands of dollars on fashionable clothes and accessories that telegraphed her beauty and sex appeal.

"No more relaxed jeans and big T-shirts," she'd declared, filling a cardboard box with most of Grace's weekend wear.

She smiled at the silk tank top and designer jeans Grace had chosen for dinner. *She's sexy as hell, and she likes it*, she thought.

"You haven't answered my question. Could we fly to South America and find the store where you bought it?"

"Honey, I doubt I could ever find that shop again. It was a total accident that I stumbled down that alley in the first place." She paused, unsure of how to say the next part. "And, truthfully, I don't think I'm supposed to find it again."

Joseph began humming eerie music and Grace smacked his arm. "What do you mean?"

She couldn't explain. They'd never talked about how she acquired the potion. The focus had always been its powers or dangers. *And that's where it needs to stay*, she thought. She could never rehash that afternoon with anyone, least of all a skeptical scientist.

She sighed and set down her wineglass. "Grace, sweetie, there's something that Joseph and I need to tell you. It's partly why we wanted to have you out for dinner."

"Oh?"

Joseph cleared his throat and squeezed her hand. "Margo asked me to test the little bit of potion that you had left in the vial."

Grace withdrew her hand and sat up straight. "What did you find?"

"It was nothing, really, mostly some benign liquids that when brought together create a chemical reaction quite pleasing to the eye."

She narrowed her eyes. "Which chemicals?"

He pulled a list from his pocket and read. "Threonine, eugenol, capsaisin and some jasmonic acid." He glanced at her, his expression serious. "There was also a slight trace of pesticide, but miniscule," he quickly added. He folded the list and returned it to his pocket. "So, while I doubt that the substance will have any long-term effects, I wouldn't recommend combing the streets of Rio for another dose."

Grace rubbed her chin, deep in thought. "Much of what you named is organic, right?"

"Yes," he said slowly. "That's why I don't believe it was harmful."

"Just let it go," Margo said. "I can't believe that potion contained pesticide! And I encouraged you to drink it. You were right all along. I never should have spiked your wine."

Grace opened her mouth to argue the point, but her cell phone chimed. She smiled and Margo knew it was Dina. *Saved by the sex goddess!*

"Hey, babe. Where are you?"

Margo glanced at Joseph, who had returned to eating his dinner. She did the same while Grace and Dina finalized their evening plans. Grace snapped her cell phone shut and scooted out of the booth.

"Sorry, but I've got to go. Dina's picking me up outside."

175

"You've hardly touched your shrimp," Margo said, pointing at her dinner.

She waved slightly, and they watched her go. After she'd exited the restaurant, they stared at each other until Joseph said, "Do you think she believed us?"

"Yes. That was quite a performance you gave," Margo said with admiration. "What the hell is all that stuff you named?"

"They are different substances, all real, and as the good doctor knows, all organic. I knew if I made shit up, she'd be suspicious. Are you sure she bought it?" he asked again. Both of them knew how easily Grace could spot a liar.

"I think so. She seemed to, at least for now. I don't know if she'll want to see that report again."

He dismissed her concern with a wave of his hand. "It won't matter. It looks very official. Besides, she's far too involved in her life. She won't give it another thought. But I still feel bad about lying to her."

"I know, but we needed to do that. She has to believe that she's in control of her life, despite the fact that you and I know she got a little help. How is your new girlfriend, anyway? Will we hear wedding bells soon?"

He grinned. "We'll see."

"We did a good thing," she concluded.

He raised his glass in salute and she joined him.

"So, did you really test the sample I gave you?"

His smile vanished, and he swallowed hard. "Yes, I tested it."

"Jesus, you look so serious. What did you find? Grace isn't going to die, is she?"

He set his glass down and stared at her. "I've been a chemist for nearly twenty years, and I've never seen anything like that potion. It derives from three substances, of this I'm sure, but whatever was in that vial has no name. It's undiscovered, and I've got no idea what it is."

A knot formed in the pit of her stomach. *What if the Root of Passion is deadly?*

"Oh, God, Joseph, what have I done?"

He wiped a hand across his face and shook his head. "As a scientist, if I was you, I'd be a little worried. The three of us have imbibed a liquid of unknown origin, and Grace drank an entire vial herself. She could drop dead at any moment."

"Thanks, I feel much better now," she snapped.

He held up a hand. "But I don't think she's in danger, honey. You're going to think I'm insane, and if I ever said this to my colleagues, I'd be fired and sent to a mental ward. When I put that slide under the microscope, I watched the blues and the reds separate and come together, over and over, and, well…"

"What?"

He gazed at her and smiled. "It looked… *friendly*."

Chapter Twenty-four

Grace zipped up her jacket to ward off the chill. It was early morning and much of nature was still asleep. The campsite was secluded, far from the highway, which minimized the possibility of human interaction. And that was what she wanted.

She followed the trail uphill, amazed that the only sounds she could hear were the crunching pine needles beneath her feet and the shrill calls of two birds high up in the trees. She trudged along slowly, admiring the rock formations, the fallen trees struck by lightning and the immense vegetation blanketing the forest floor. Everything had bloomed a few months prior, and the morning hike was a gift she relished with each step.

The trail veered right, but twenty yards to the left an enormous flat rock jutted from the side of the mountain, creating a makeshift overlook. She perched on the rock and stared down at the wall of trees that surrounded the valley below. Mist swirled like a steaming cauldron, obstructing her view of the basin. She closed her eyes, allowing her senses to overwhelm her. She inhaled deeply, the morning air filling her lungs, making her dizzy. It was almost as intoxicating as the Root of Passion.

After the evening with Margo and Joseph she'd never mentioned the potion again. She realized that regardless of its origin, to replicate the effects continuously would make her an addict, just like someone who couldn't survive without alcohol, meth, or pharmaceuticals. Still, she missed that feeling of the river rushing past her, giving her the courage to face her fears. And she needed that courage now.

She had to make a decision, one that could change her life. She'd hoped that coming to the mountains—alone—would help her see clearly, but the mist over the valley seemed symbolic and aptly timed. She reached for the satellite phone attached to her belt and hit speed dial one.

"Hey," a sleepy voice said.

"Hey, yourself. Did I wake you?"

"Yeah, but that's okay. You're up on the rock, right?"

Grace smiled at her intuitiveness. "Yes. I'm thinking."

"Good. You need to think. Did you have any trouble with the tent?"

"No, it went right up. Everything's been great."

"I'm glad. Is there a specific reason you called? Have you had any epiphanies you'd like to share?"

"I just wanted to hear your voice. I'm hanging up now."

Penny laughed. "That's just tortuous, Grace. Thanks a lot. You wake me up just to tease me. When are you coming back?"

She let the question hang in the air and watched the mist roll over the valley. "I'm due back at work on Tuesday."

"Oh."

They both knew the implications. She could either spend another day alone in the mountains and drive back to Penny's for a quick unloading of the camping gear she'd borrowed, or she could drive back today, and they could spend time together—

something they'd avoided since her last trip to Vegas.

"I'll call you later, okay?"

"Sure."

"Penny, are you angry?" she thought to ask.

"No, I'm not. Really. You believe me, don't you?"

She did. If Penny was anything, she was the most sincere and honest person Grace had ever met.

"Okay, 'bye." She disconnected and stared into the valley. Floating high above the tree line, she felt powerful, omnipotent. *Of course, you had to four-wheel in Penny's Jeep the whole way here, Grace. How God-like does that make you?*

Penny. What to do? Their connection had started innocently when Grace had Googled Linus McWhirter's address and returned her clothes. They began exchanging e-mails. At first, they discussed the unbelievable weekend and Logan's outrageous behavior, but then, without realizing it, the flower of trust opened, and one comment linked to another, until they were friends. She had no idea when it happened; although if she reviewed all of Penny's e-mails, which she kept in a folder, she knew she could trace the evolution of their relationship.

Somehow, though, that no longer seemed important. Much of their initial correspondence revolved around Dina, who, after four months, disappeared one night, leaving a note for Grace in her mailbox detailing her plan to work in a surf shop in Ocean Beach, California. At first she'd been devastated, but it was Penny who pulled her from the malaise and she found herself hurrying home each night and firing up her computer to see Penny's latest e-mail, which always made her laugh or think. Penny was as intelligent as she was funny, and Grace knew she'd be a wonderful psychologist.

Once in a while they spoke on the phone, but they shared the same disdain for small talk, and the awkward pauses eventually led to an agreement that e-mail was their best form of communication. Eventually Penny asked Grace to return to Las Vegas for a camping trip. One weekend led to another, and another. It was at the end of their third trip a month before that the relationship unexpectedly shifted. When they went to exchange a friendly kiss on the cheek at the airport, the corners of their lips brushed together, and the kiss lingered far longer than it should have. Grace had spent the entire flight home thinking of that moment and reliving the tenderness of Penny's mouth, one she'd never felt against her own.

Of course, they'd talked about the kiss and their feelings in the e-mails that followed. Honesty and candor created the comfort in their relationship, and Penny admitted that she wanted more—much more. She'd been accepted to Arizona State and UC San Diego, and she'd told Grace that she'd go to ASU if it meant they would give their relationship a shot.

She reached into her pocket and withdrew the battered photograph of her and Penny at the wedding. She'd removed it from the photo album months ago and kept it by the computer. She'd received an invitation to Logan's show in New York, which featured her latest and greatest photo, *Moment of Grace*, but of course she didn't go. It would have been far too embarrassing.

For the hundredth time in the last day, she gazed at the picture. Penny's soul was in her smile, and whenever Grace stared at her she sighed, thinking of her kind heart. She'd ignored her during the wild weekend, too enamored with Logan and dazzled by Lena to really see her.

She peered over the edge of the rock, noting the sharp drop toward the valley. It felt like her life. Should she leap or remain safely planted on solid ground? If she had the Root of Passion, she knew exactly what she'd do, but this decision wasn't just about her. Penny was potentially altering her life for Grace. *No pressure there, Grace.* She wasn't sure she could handle that responsibility.

She should tell Penny that she didn't know if it would work. Then Penny would make her own choices—and perhaps choose San Diego. *Maybe she'll run into Dina.* That thought sparked jealousy, as irrational as it was. Still, wherever Penny went, the doctoral program would consume her life, and Grace knew the probability of seeing her was minimal if she was far away. And if she chose San Diego, she would likely relocate there after graduation. *How do you feel about losing her? What if she wasn't in your life—at all?*

She pulled the phone out and dialed.

Penny chuckled when she answered. "That was quick. You're not lost, are you?"

"No, but I do have a few questions."

"Okay," Penny said hesitantly. "What?"

"Are you still in bed?"

"Uh-huh. And I'm alone, in case you wanted clarification."

She laughed. "That's good to know. So, my next question is, when you're lying in bed, can you see the Pollock?"

There was a long pause, and she heard Penny sigh deeply. "Yes, Grace, I can see the Pollock from here, and every time I look at it I think of you. I told you I was rather ambivalent toward it when my dad got it for me, but now I totally love it."

She wondered if Penny had any idea that she was grinning from ear to ear. "Thanks. That's all I wanted. 'Bye."

She pulled the tattered note paper from her pocket and read through Michelle and Margo's infamous list once more. Number five still remained undone. *You know how you feel about loose ends, Grace.* She closed her eyes and lay down on the rock. The sky was a rich blue, not as deep as the cerulean that swirled in the Root of Passion, but beautiful nonetheless. She slowed her breathing, envisioning the intricate pathways of her body that she knew so well as a surgeon, imagining the Root of Passion swirling inside her.

And, unexpectedly, the river appeared again, roaring over her prostrate body, pressing her deeper into her rocky perch. Eventually she opened her eyes, rejuvenated and bold. She held up the picture and the list once more—and leaped.

Chapter Twenty-five

Margo wandered the streets of Rio until she found the familiar marketplace—at least she thought it was the right one. A year had passed since she'd purchased the Root of Passion. So much had happened—because of that.

Joseph had married Ainsley, and they were expecting a child. Grace and Penny were living in Grace's bungalow, nesting and building a life together. Margo had never seen her so happy.

She sighed. While the potion had greatly improved the lives of her friends and brought momentary joy to the one person she'd loved, it wasn't powerful enough to reverse death.

Rose had died four months ago. On her deathbed, she called Margo and asked if she was able to fly into New York—the first time she'd ever requested her presence. She cancelled her next flight and was at her bedside for the last few days of her life.

Her family only asked a few questions, but the hand-holding and frequent references to "my darling," or "my love," must have given them a clue. When Rose finally slipped away as the sun set one evening, they invited Margo to the service, but she declined. She did, though, visit the cemetery each time she flew into New York.

The worst part had been the silent grief. She realized that since she'd excluded Grace and Joseph from celebrating her love for Rose, they must remain ignorant of her death. Otherwise they would be hurt and offended that she'd kept something so important from them. So she wept in private, determined to revel in their newfound happiness—that she had created for them. While each day was punctuated with constant thoughts of Rose, she recognized her emotions weren't as raw, and plodding through life was growing easier.

She stopped walking. Lost in her thoughts, she'd paid no attention to where her feet directed her, and now she found herself standing in front of the green door.

"Shit."

She glanced about the alley, recognizing the bizarre black-and-white drawings in each of the windows. When she took a deep breath, vanilla filled her senses. Indeed, it was the same place. She put her hands on her hips and sighed, unable to fathom how she'd arrived here. Just that morning she'd thought of the marketplace and tried to remember the route to the store—and she couldn't.

Maybe you just needed to see it, or maybe your conscious mind isn't at work here.

She stepped into the shop and glanced at the walls of potions. Nothing had changed. As she studied the beautiful bottles and carafes, she saw potions she hadn't noticed the first time. She'd been in awe of the discovery and unable to notice the details. Also, it was much different now that she was a believer. *Did all of the potions have the same power as the Root of Passion?*

Footsteps sounded behind her, and she closed her eyes,

hoping.

"I see you have returned."

She smiled and faced the goddess, Chayna. Her voice wasn't as Margo remembered, but her incredible face and figure could have been cast in bronze.

"I'm not really sure how I got here, and I don't know why I'm here. I don't intend to buy any more potions."

"You don't need to. You are, what would you say, a satisfied customer."

"I guess," she replied, but she thought of Rose's grave, and tears pooled in her eyes. She looked away, staring at a tiny glass box labeled, *Anger Control*. When she'd collected herself, she said, "Um, I'm sorry to have bothered you. I should be going."

"Do you want to know why you're here?" Chayna asked before she could move.

"I thought it was an accident."

"No."

Chayna went to a shelf and removed the familiar tire-like bottle. "Do you remember this?"

"Yes, you asked me to drink it, and I did. You said you wouldn't give me the second Root of Passion if I didn't."

Chayna nodded and handed her the bottle. "Raise it up and read the label on the bottom."

She squinted, barely able to make out the tiny letters. "Revolution. For a safe return." She shook her head. "I'm a little thick. I don't get it."

"The bottle is a circle, equaling three-hundred and sixty degrees—"

"It starts and ends in the same place, or one revolution. You gave me this potion so I could come back."

"Exactly."

"Why?"

Chayna didn't answer. She replaced the bottle and led Margo into the back room.

What she found was a simple living area with a small kitchenette and a bed. Across the room was a stuffed sofa, facing an easel. Chayna stood next to it, motioning to the tablet perched on the easel. She went behind her—and dropped her purse. Staring at her was a charcoal portrait of Rose.

"How do you know her?"

"I don't. She came to me in a dream, and the image was so strong that I jumped from my bed and ran to the easel. The next day you walked into my shop."

She couldn't believe what she was hearing. "You drew this picture before you even knew me? How can that be?"

"It is not for us to understand. I only knew that this person was important. When you showed up and started talking about your friend, Grace, at first I thought it was her. Then, after you requested the second vial, and so readily drank the black potion, I knew this wasn't Grace. This was someone much more important to you."

She stared into the charcoal eyes. Chayna had completely captured Rose's most important feature, and her knees went weak. Chayna set her on the stool before she fell to the floor.

"I'm sorry if I've caused you grief. I hope the Root of Passion helped. Did it?"

"Yes," she said softly. "She felt things she'd never felt before... before she died."

Chayna touched her shoulder. "I'm sorry. I thought that might be the case, but you must focus on the joy she discovered—that you helped her to find. You enriched her life in a way no one else could."

A thought occurred to her. "I'm still confused. You said that you knew she was important to me when I came into the shop. But how did you know she belonged to me? How did you know *me*?"

Chayna smiled slightly. "That's a very good question."

She moved to another part of the room, to an open cabinet filled with tablets. She randomly grabbed three of them and brought them to the bed.

"Please look."

Margo flipped open the first book to a pen and ink sketch of a man sitting at a table. The second page, done in pastels, displayed a beautiful field of flowers.

"That's beautiful."

"Thank you."

The third page was a wild pencil drawing with little form. She could tell it was a naked woman, lying on a couch. She was about to ask what these drawings had to do with her, when she randomly flipped deeper into the tablet—and saw the same picture, only with more form. The simple pencil lines were replaced with bold charcoal strokes, and the figure seemed oddly familiar to her.

Flipping ahead several pages, she saw more pastoral scenes and pen and ink drawings, but interspersed were pictures of the woman. Her face was always in profile and without form, but she was in different scenes—shopping, eating at a café and bathing.

She reached for the second book, which was much like the first, but she could see more detail to the woman's face—particularly her eyes. Whereas most of the drawings from the first book showed her face at an angle, in the second tablet, she faced forward.

How do I know her?

While she admired Chayna's talent, she was tired of the exercise. She picked up the third tablet and flipped to a page near the back—and froze. The haphazard pencil drawing from the first book was fully transposed to an incredible black and white charcoal drawing—of her. She lay on the very couch that sat five feet away, her body relaxed, but posed. One hand rested behind her head, while the other draped across her belly. She wore a slight smile, as if she was enjoying the attention. In the corner of the drawing sat a figure at an easel.

"What? How?"

"Again, I can't explain it. I've been dreaming of you for a long time. Look at the date on the back. I drew this picture three years ago. When I saw your friend in my dream, and then I met you, well, I knew everything was connected. And while I wanted to help you and your friends, I wanted to see you again. Perhaps that was selfish."

She closed the tablets and returned them to the cabinet. Margo was speechless. Who was this woman? Should she be terrified or thrilled? It was too much to process.

"I need to go. I really can't deal with this right now."

Chayna nodded in resignation. "I understand. I've known of my dreams for quite some time, but you've had only this moment to grasp the unthinkable. I hope you will consider coming back in the future. I'd like to know the real you, not just the one I imagine."

"Perhaps."

Chayna's smile broadened. "If you would agree to drink the potion again, your return would be guaranteed."

She stiffened, unwilling to make such a commitment. She paused, choosing her words carefully. "I don't think I can. Perhaps the last dose will stay with me. That's a possibility, isn't it?" She hoped she sounded optimistic.

Chayna looked away. "There are always possibilities."

She left quickly, slamming the green door on the way out. She bent over in the alley, catching her breath. She felt light-headed, and everything seemed to be spinning. When she could walk a straight line, she headed back into the noisy marketplace, grateful to return to the chaos of real life.

That shop is a fantasy. It doesn't exist. It isn't real.

She wandered amid the buyers and sellers, their voices feverish to make a deal. Laughter and music were everywhere, but a flash of red caught her attention. An old woman sat on the ground holding a bright red bowl. She was apart from the vendors, and she gazed into a distance, ignoring everything around her. Margo moved closer and saw that her lips were moving, forming words she couldn't hear. She wore an old brown dress that exposed her splintery arms. She held the bowl between her gnarled hands lovingly and carefully, as if it were the only possession in the world that mattered. Margo saw that other shoppers had dropped Brazilian reais and even some U.S. dollars into the bowl.

Moved by the image of true suffering, she pulled some reais from her purse and leaned over the bowl. The woman's bad breath tickled her nostrils, and she heard pieces of the endless monologue, although she didn't understand Portuguese.

As her money clinked against the ceramic, the monologue paused, and she thought the old woman said, "Go back," before she resumed her endless chatter.

She stood straight up as if she'd been bitten. Her heart pounded in her chest and she stepped backward, running into a display of pots. She apologized to the angry vendor and quickly headed down another aisle, away from the woman and her jibberish.

This is real, isn't it? Isn't it?

She leaned against the nearest wall and closed her eyes, allowing the sounds of the marketplace to wash over her. When she opened her eyes, she paid no mind to her feet and only listened to the music and laughter as she weaved through the endless aisles.

Minutes later she was once again in front of the green door. She pressed her hand against the wood. It was warm from the sun's kiss.

This is real.

She found Chayna in the back room at her easel, her left hand holding a piece of charcoal. When their eyes met, she froze.

"I was hoping you would come back."

"I guess the potion was strong enough," Margo said.

Chayna chuckled as she crossed the room. "I would hope so. I gave you a double dose." She caressed her cheek. Her hand was warm and soothing. "I'd like to share with you another dream I had recently."

"Yes."

She pulled Margo to her and kissed her softly. And Margo knew it was real.

SIDE ORDER OF LOVE by Tracey Richardson. Television foodie star Grace Wellwood is not going to be golf phenom Torrie Cannon's side order of romance for the summer tour. No, she's not. Absolutely not. $13.95

WORTH EVERY STEP by KG MacGregor. Climbing Africa's highest peak isn't nearly so hard as coming back down to earth. Join two women who risk their futures and hearts on the journey of their lives. $13.95

WHACKED by Josie Gordon. Death by family values. Lonnie Squires knows that if they'd warned her about this possibility in seminary, she'd remember. $13.95

BECKA'S SONG by Frankie J. Jones. Mysterious, beautiful women with secrets are to be avoided. Leanne Dresher knows it with her head, but her heart has other plans. Becka James is simply unavoidable. 13.95

GETTING THERE by Lyn Denison. Kat knows her life needs fixing. She just doesn't want to go to the one place where she can do that: home. $13.95

PARTNERS by Gerri Hill. Detective Casey O'Connor has had difficult cases, but what she needs most from fellow detective Tori Hunter is help understanding her new partner, Leslie Tucker. 13.95

AS FAR AS FAR ENOUGH by Claire Rooney. Two very different women from two very different worlds meet by accident—literally. Collier and Meri find their love threatened on all sides. There's only one way to survive: together. $13.95